# SKIP

## BY AILEEN FISHER

*Illustrated by Wayne Blickenstaff*

SCHOLASTIC BOOK SERVICES

Published by Scholastic Book Services, a division
of Scholastic Magazines, Inc., New York, N.Y.

*Other Books by Aileen Fisher:*

A Lantern in the Window
All on a Mountain Day
Summer of Little Rain
My Cousin Abe

To

*Everyone Who Loves a Dog*

Single copy price 35¢.

Quantity prices available on request.

1st printing . . . . . . . . . . . . . March 1963

# CONTENTS

# 1  The Day it Happened

Krissy would never forget that day in January. The day Eric and Dad went to the Stock Show in Denver. "You never know what's going to happen until it happens," she thought afterward. "And then it's too late. Oh, Skip! Skip!"

She came home on the school bus feeling all bright inside, like the sun blazing on the snow. She was to have a part in the Valentine play. She was to be the Queen of Hearts who patched up broken hearts and made them whole again, like new!

Sitting next to her best friend, Sharon Peterson, Krissy talked and laughed. "Isn't it *bright?*" she said, nodding toward the window. "Look, Sharon. White snow, green pines on the hills, blue sky — my favorite, favorite colors!" Oh, everything was favorite today.

Krissy wished she could climb the big hill with Skip when she got home. The view would be wonderful on a day like this, when everything was so sparkling inside and out. But there wouldn't be time today, not with Eric and Dad gone and extra chores to do. How white the peaks of the Rockies would look, though, against the blue sky, beyond miles of humpy foothills!

"Colorado's prettiest in winter with sun on the snow," Sharon was agreeing. She was always so slow, like winter molasses. "But if you had to look at the glare all day, you'd go snow-blind, Krissy."

"Would I?"

"Well, some people do."

"But cows don't, Sharon. And they're outside all day."

"Maybe animals are different," Sharon said.

"Skip's different — *all* ways!" Krissy exclaimed fondly. Then suddenly she giggled. "Do you know he's younger than I am, even though he's three times as old?"

Sharon gave her a blank look.

"It's true."

"You're past eleven," Sharon said sturdily. "How can Skip be three times as old?"

"Dad says that one year for us counts for seven with a dog. So Skip's thirty-five! But he doesn't act like it, does he?" She had to smile. Sharon sometimes had the funniest look on her face, with her mouth half open.

"Then Trigger must be . . . let's see . . ." Sharon paused to figure it out. "Almost twelve," she decided after a long silence. "Just like me."

But Krissy hardly heard. She was back with the Queen of Hearts, acting out her part for Valentine's Day. Would

Verna let her wear her full red skirt? Krissy wondered. She'd have to pin it over, but it would be so bright and cheerful for a Queen of Hearts. "I can sew red hearts on my new white blouse," she said aloud.

Sharon gave her that look again.

"For the play," Krissy explained. "And I'll make a cardboard crown covered with gold paper, and maybe Eric will put in some shiny rivets for jewels."

Gaily Krissy jumped off the bus when it stopped at the Ohlings' gate. Her older sister Verna stepped off more primly. Today there were only the two of them getting off, for Eric was in Denver at the National Western Stock Show. It was Eric's big day. He was going to try for a catch-it calf. If he could catch and hold onto one, put on a halter and lead it out of the arena, it would be his.

Verna stopped to get the mail from the battered box with faded lettering. She was sixteen, and she answered ads in the farm magazines and wrote letters to pen pals and to "Teen-age Troubles" columns. She was always sending for samples and catalogues and premiums. Every afternoon she looked in the mailbox expectantly.

"Look, Verna!" Krissy tried to jump over the old ridge of snow the snowplow had left. "Look. I'm the Queen of Hearts." She sprawled in the snowbank.

"You look more like a catch-it calf to me," Verna remarked loftily. "C grade. And if you get all wet, you'll catch it for sure." She picked her way down the track Dad's truck had made.

Krissy shook the snow out of her mitts. Oh, Verna! Her head was full of needles and thread. No wonder she said so many pricky things. All she liked to do when she came home from school was sew, sew, sew. She was even doing some sewing for Mrs. Peterson now, for pay.

Brushing herself off and shaking the snow from her blond braids, Krissy called gaily to Skip. He was trotting up the lane to meet her, the way he always did. "Here, Skip! Skip!"

Oh, he was beautiful in the sunlight. The tan part of his coat was like living gold, with some of it spilling over into the white of his collar. And his tail! Krissy could never get over the way Skip held his tail, curved up over his back like a showery white waterfall. And she was always surprised at the way his hair parted in a straight line down the middle of his back.

He wasn't really Krissy's dog. He belonged to the whole family. But he *was* really her dog, too, because she loved him most. Dad was always too busy with the ranch and the cows. Mom had five children and Dad and two hundred chickens to look after, so she couldn't think much about Skip. She never forgot to feed him, but she was too busy to play with him or pet him.

Eric had his 4-H Club projects. And now if he caught a catch-it calf, he'd have that too. And Verna! There wasn't any room for Skip in the midst of all her patterns and dress goods. Krissy sometimes wondered how it must look inside Verna's head, with patterns going this way and that.

As for Annie and Carl, they were so young — only five and three — that they lived in a little world of their own. Sometimes their world included Skip, but not often. Mostly they lived in a pod that held only two peas, Krissy thought — a bigger pea and a littler one.

Yes, when you came right down to it, Skip was *hers* more than anyone else's. She loved everything about him. He was such fun, always so eager and full of life. He had a way of smiling all around his mouth, and he even laughed sometimes, out loud.

And brave! That was one of the biggest things about Skip. He wasn't afraid of anything — dogs twice his size, cows, horses, snakes, people. Krissy remembered the time she and Eric had passed a cabin in the hills when they were looking for raspberries. Six big dogs came dashing out, barking furiously, lunging and snapping. Krissy felt herself go weak, and even Eric turned pale. But not Skip! He trotted right up to the angry dogs, his tail waving high, and made friends.

That's the way Skip was — acting out what he wasn't able to put into words: "Don't be afraid. Don't run from danger. Face up to it. If you turn tail, the danger follows you. Face up to it, Krissy. Face up to it, Eric. Don't be afraid."

Krissy scooped up a handful of snow, made a soft

snowball, and threw it. "Catch it, Skip! Get it!" But he was too busy sniffing around an old wild currant bush to notice. Maybe Trigger had been around, or a strange dog. She threw another snowball. Funny, Skip didn't seem to want to run after them any more, the way he used to. He used to run and jump and catch them in his mouth. It couldn't be that he was getting too old to play, even though he was "thirty-five." No, Skip would never be that old.

She ran after him and caught hold of him, digging her fingers gently into the deep fur of his neck. He stopped his sniffing and rubbed his head against her. She was so proud of him. He was the only border collie for miles around. "He's small for a collie," she would explain when anyone asked. "The way a Shetland pony is small for a horse."

She began to run down the track. "Race with the Queen of Hearts, Skip," she called.

The Queen of Hearts! How could Krissy know what was to happen to her heart before the day was over?

When she ran into the house to take off her school dress and get into her jeans, Mom was talking on the phone. Her voice filled the kitchen with surprise. "Really? You don't say! Oh, how wonderful."

Krissy pumped herself a drink at the kitchen sink. Annie and Carl came galloping into the kitchen like a team of horses, and Krissy shushed them, eager to hear what was so wonderful at the other end of the wire.

"Colored fixtures!" Mom exclaimed. "Green tile! Oh, Grace."

Grace. Then it was Mrs. Craghorn, a mile up the road on the old Watkins place. Mr. Craghorn worked in town. He ran some range cows on the ranch, but he made his money in town, working in a garage. So they were going to add a bathroom! Krissy rinsed out the glass and set it upside down on the drainboard.

"It's the dream of my life to have a bathroom someday," Mom was saying. "But I suppose I'll be gray-haired before I get one."

Krissy looked at Mom quickly. Her hair was light brown and wavy, like Verna's. It had flickers of red when she stood at the window against the light. There wasn't a sign of gray. Would she have to wait so long for a bathroom? So long as that?

Verna came from the living room and stood in the doorway, listening. "I'd settle for an electric sewing machine," she said, mostly to herself. "That's the dream of *my* life."

"I try to save something out of the egg money each week," Mom was telling Mrs. Craghorn. "But you'd be surprised how little there is left. Always something to be bought right away. I probably couldn't even buy a faucet with what I've saved so far. But I think it's wonderful you're going to have a bathroom, Grace."

"I want a pony," Annie said. "All my own."

"Me too," said Carl.

"Someday I hope we *all* get what we want," Mom was saying. "At least, we have a pump at the kitchen sink. Well, good-bye, Grace. Bring over the plans some afternoon." She hung up.

Krissy thought Mom's face looked flushed, as if she had been leaning over the stove. But it's only the flush of her dream, Krissy decided. Then aloud: "Is it really the dream of your life, Mom?"

"What, Krissy?"

"A bathroom."

"Well, yes, I guess it is." Mom gave a little laugh. "But it doesn't keep me awake at night, worrying about it."

Krissy went into the bedroom she shared with Verna and Annie. Thoughtfully she took off her school clothes. There was Dad wanting to build up a good herd. And Eric wanting to go to the state college of agriculture when he finished high school. And Verna yearning for an electric sewing machine. And Annie and Carl talking about ponies.

"I haven't any great wish," Krissy thought. "I like things just the way they are — the folks, the ranch, and Skip. I hope they don't change, that's all."

No, Krissy didn't have any great wish right then. Not until later. Just a little later . . .

# 2        In the Haymow

K RISSY PUT ON HER WRAPS and started for the door. "I'm going to play with Skip while the sun's still up," she said. "It's so bright and shiny out and full of sparkles."

Mom looked up from the clothes she was dampening. "Bring some wood for the kitchen stove, will you, Krissy? And some coal in the bucket. Not too much at a time, though. Eric won't be home to do his chores tonight, you know."

"Do you think he'll catch a calf, Mom?"

"Oh, I hope so. If he's lucky, he will."

"He's been lucky so far," Krissy said. "There were a lot of 4-H boys wanting to enter the contest."

"Yes, there must have been. It was open to boys from six states, wasn't it? Colorado, Wyoming . . . Kansas . . ."

"Nebraska, New Mexico, and Oklahoma," Krissy finished. "So many applied they had to draw lots."

"Eric was lucky his number was drawn," Mom nodded.

"And he's lucky Dad could take him to Denver in the truck, so they'll have a way to bring the calf home."

Mom laughed. "You aren't putting the truck before the calf, are you, Krissy?"

"I'm lucky, too," Krissy told Skip as she headed for the shed. "Today's my lucky day. I'm Queen of Hearts!" She saw the Petersons' little black-and-white terrier cutting across the field. "Here comes your friend Trigger, Skip. Here's where you get a good run."

She liked to see Skip play with Trigger, dash after him, and chase him with make-believe anger. Skip always acted as if he didn't like other dogs to come near the house, but he didn't really mind. He just wanted them to know who owned this ranch and the buildings and the folks who lived here.

But today Skip didn't seem to notice he had company. Not until he caught Trigger's scent. Then he lifted his head with a jerk, and the hair on his back went up.

Trigger darted in closer, wanting to play. He was smaller than Skip, and quick like a bird, Krissy thought, with those slender white legs. Trigger liked to run up close, edging in, and then dash off just in the nick of time. Skip would chase him around the yard, around the barn, and finally right out to the road.

Today, though, something was wrong. Skip began running in circles that didn't have anything to do with Trigger. Krissy watched, amused. Skip looked so funny. "Catch him, Skip! Catch him," she urged.

Skip kept circling like crazy.

Trigger came teasing-in, closer than usual. Then he sat on his haunches and waited, one ear up and the other flopped down. He cocked his head. He didn't know what to make of Skip, either.

Krissy began to laugh. Skip acting like that, going around and around like a clown, and the Petersons' dog sitting there trying to figure it out!

The shine on the snow — that was it. Although the sun was getting low in the winter sky as it dipped toward the foothills, the last burst of dazzle must be blinding Skip. Snow-blind! Of course. Why *couldn't* animals go snow-blind? Krissy could make her eyes into slits and squint right into the sun. She did it now. But Skip wouldn't know about squinting.

Finally Trigger trotted off without being chased. Skip kept sniffing around for his tracks. "You're a funny dog," Krissy said, and went to get the wood and coal for Mom.

After the woodbox was full, and the coal bucket shoved out of sight behind the stove, Mom sent Krissy to the barn to pitch down hay for the milk cows. "While you can still see up there in the loft," Mom said. "Mr. Peterson's coming over to help with the milking, but I don't want to take too much of his time. He has enough work of his own. So if you'll throw down the hay, Krissy, it will be a big help. You know how much. You've seen Eric and Dad do it."

Yes, Krissy knew. Skip followed her to the barn, right

up the narrow stairs to the mow. She had to close her eyes for a moment in order to see in the half-dark. The mow was a big, dusky place on a late-winter afternoon.

She found the pitchfork and began throwing forkfuls of hay down the chute to the cow barn. There were five milk cows. They would need quite a bit of hay. The seventy range cows back in the hills didn't have to be milked, or fed very often. Dad hauled hay to them only when the ground was covered with snow.

She pitched another forkful. The Queen of Hearts pitching hay! She smiled. "Whoops, watch out there, Skip!" Half a forkful of hay broke away from the rest and fell on Skip's head. He backed away, shaking himself.

The mow smelled good — dry and fragrant, as if a piece of summer had been hidden there away from the snow and cold. Krissy leaned on the pitchfork and sniffed and watched the hay dust twinkle in the shaft of light that came through a high window.

Something dark like a shadow brushed against her leg, brushed back again. Something made a happy bumbling-rumbling sound. "Why, Blackie!" Krissy exclaimed. "Where did you come from?" She glanced at Skip before bending down to stroke the old cat's back and ears. Skip was always jealous when she petted Blackie or Tom. But now, although he had his head turned toward Krissy, Skip didn't seem to mind.

"Nice Blackie," Krissy said, watching Skip.

He was sniffing this way and that, his nostrils twitching. He could smell the cat, all right. The hair on his back was up. But, strangely enough, he didn't rush at Blackie the way he usually did when she was getting attention. He went toward the chute instead.

Krissy noticed how thin Blackie looked. "I bet you've had kittens again," she said. Blackie kept brushing against Krissy's jeans, purring. "If I don't take any more notice of her," Krissy thought, "perhaps she'll go back to her nest. Then I can find the kittens."

It worked. Krissy found the cat's hide-out behind the chute to the box stall. There were four squirming little ones, squeaking and squealing in thin voices. They were only a few days old.

"I won't tell Dad," Krissy promised the mother cat. "But he'll probably find them . . . he always does. And then there'll just be you and Tom again."

Dad didn't want cats-all-over-the-place. That's what he said: "Cats-all-over-the-place."

She pitched down a few extra forkfuls for good measure, while Skip waited for her in the shadows. "All right, Skip," she said finally. "Come on, I'll race you down the stairs."

But Skip didn't want to race.

"Come on!"

She started clattering down the steps. Skip stayed at the top, waiting, hesitating.

"Skip! What's the matter with you?" Krissy was at the bottom now, looking up. "Come on."

And then it happened. Skip tried to obey. He tried to come. He put out his foot, but he missed. He fell. Down, down he tumbled, bumping one step after another.

Krissy rushed to catch him. "Why, Skip, what happened? You've come down the stairs dozens of times. What's the matter, boy?" She threw her arms around him and held him safe on the fourth step from the bottom. "You're all right, aren't you? You didn't get hurt?"

Skip whimpered a little and leaned against her. He seemed to want to stay there leaning against her, bowing his head. Krissy braced herself on the narrow step and rubbed him and patted him. Then slowly she helped him down to the door where the light came in.

"You just slipped," she said.

Skip stared straight ahead, his ears drooping, his head down.

Krissy put out her hand to rub his nose, and then she noticed something for the first time. Skip didn't blink. Even when she put her hand close to his eyes, he didn't blink. That was queer. Was he still snow-blind?

Kneeling on the cold threshold, she looked into the little collie's eyes. She hadn't really looked for a long time. She knew his eyes were brown, golden brown. But now there seemed to be a blue film over them. Completely over them.

The awful truth dawned on her. Oh, Skip! Skip! He hadn't gone snow-blind. He had gone *real* blind. Skip couldn't see. He couldn't *see*.

Krissy's own eyes began to mist over. Her throat tightened till it hurt. She could hardly swallow. Something warm was running down her cheeks. Oh, Skip! She knew what Dad would say.

"Animals on this ranch have to pay their way," Dad would say. "We can't afford to keep them if they don't pay their way. Not with the price we're getting for beef these days. Not with the long drought cutting our crops in half. Not with taxes high as they are. No, sir."

Oh, Skip!

When Dad put the cows in the pasture that took in the house and barn, it was Skip's job to keep them away from Mom's flowers and shrubs. To keep them away from the row of Chinese elms Dad had planted for a windbreak. Otherwise the cows would strip off the leaves. How could Skip do his job now . . . now that he couldn't see?

Dad kept records on the cows, and Mom kept records on the chickens, and Eric kept records on his 4-H Club projects. Everything had to pay its way. What would they think of a dog who couldn't see!

"But you're still Skip," Krissy choked into the white fur collar. "That hasn't changed. You're still Skip."

She took out her handkerchief and wiped her eyes and blew her nose. She mustn't go on crying. Mom or Verna would notice and ask questions. And Krissy wasn't going to tell. She wouldn't tell! Because if the folks knew, they might send Skip away. It would be the way it always was with Blackie's kittens. One day they would be there squeaking in the nest. And the next day they'd be gone.

She ran a gentle finger up and down the white line on Skip's nose. "It's a good thing you aren't a house dog," she said. "They'd notice more." Skip was an outside dog, and always had been. Dad had cut a hole in the barn and nailed a flap of gunny sacks over it, so Skip could go in and out when the weather was cold or rainy.

Krissy clung to the little collie. She had loved him from the very first, but now she loved him more than ever. Now that he was blind, she'd watch over him like a mother hen. He needed her. She'd get him used to knowing where things were without seeing them. She'd put maps in his head, the way Verna had patterns in hers.

"It isn't as if you *done* anything, Skip," she whispered. "Killed one of Mom's chickens or something. It isn't as if it's your *fault*."

But it wasn't the kittens' fault, either, was it?

Lovingly, she held her cold fingers over Skip's eyes. She put her cheek against her fingers. "We won't tell anyone," she promised. "It'll be our secret."

# 3        The Queen of Hearts

K RISSY DIDN'T FEEL LIKE HERSELF at supper. She could hardly eat. She could hardly get anything past the lump that blocked her throat. And she was afraid to talk, for fear her voice would wobble. Skip! Skip! "I mustn't let on," she thought. "I mustn't let them think anything is wrong." For once she hoped that Verna would have a new pattern to talk to Mom about.

How different the whole world looked all of a sudden. She had planned to tell about the Queen of Hearts at suppertime. The Queen of Hearts! What did it mean now? What did it matter if Verna would let her wear the red skirt? Somebody else would have to play the part now. Krissy couldn't go through with it.

She blinked back the mist that kept coming before her eyes. "What did you and Carl do today?" she asked Annie, when Verna went to get the samples of dress goods that had come in the mail.

Annie was only too glad to tell. "We played school.

And, Krissy, what do you think? Carlie can read *The Three Bears* upside down! And then after we played school, we made a house out of the kitchen chairs, and Mom let me wear her shoes . . ."

But Krissy wasn't listening.

Krissy knew one prayer, "Now I Lay Me," but she didn't always remember to say it. Usually she fell asleep so quickly after crawling into the double bed beside Annie that there wasn't time to remember anything. Verna had a cot in the same room, the bedroom off the living room to the west. But Krissy never heard her come to bed.

Tonight was different. Krissy wasn't sleepy. She kept thinking about Skip. He was used to being alone out in the dark barn at night. But tomorrow and tomorrow and tomorrow he'd be in the dark in the *daytime*, too.

"I'll be with him all the time I can," Krissy told herself. "So he won't feel alone. So he'll know somebody cares."

Outside, a bitter January wind had begun to blow, and the bedroom was as cold as the meat locker down at the feed store. Cold, even with the window closed. Krissy scrunched under the covers and put her feet against Annie's legs. Annie didn't know there was more than weather to make a person cold tonight!

"Now I lay me . . ." Krissy began. Then she stopped. Maybe if she knelt by the bed, instead of being muffled under the covers, the Lord would pay more attention. She slipped out onto the braided rag rug Mom had made, and knelt in the cold. She hesitated. That wasn't the right prayer for tonight. Tonight it should be about Skip.

"Dear God," she began slowly. "You probably know about Skip already, because you know about everything. Can't you make Dad see that it isn't Skip's fault — that he's still a good dog? He's the best dog I'll ever have. He's the only one I want. Amen."

Shivering, she slipped back to bed, close to Annie. Would he hear? Would he have room in his heart for a dog? Oh yes, Krissy assured herself — for a dog like Skip.

The next morning Krissy was glad Eric and Dad were still at the Stock Show, because that meant everyone was unusually busy. Even with Mr. Peterson coming to help with the milking, there were many extra little chores for everyone except Carl. No one had time to notice how anyone felt — not even Mom, who usually noticed right away.

Sitting beside Sharon on the school bus, Krissy found it hard not to tell her secret. Sharon would be sorry, because she thought Skip was beautiful, too. But she might blurt out something in front of Verna.

"I'm not going to be the Queen of Hearts," Krissy said finally.

Sharon looked at her in dismay. "You aren't! Why not? You're the best one."

"I don't feel like it any more."

Sharon couldn't believe it. She was so surprised she

even talked faster. Like molasses in March instead of January. "But, Krissy, you felt like it *yesterday*."

"Something happened," Krissy said, trying to hold her voice steady. "It's a secret. I mustn't tell. I'm going to ask Mrs. Steele to pick someone else."

She stood at Mrs. Steele's desk before the last gong sounded. "I can't play the Queen of Hearts," she said simply.

"You can't, Kristine? Doesn't your mother want you to? I should have told you . . . you won't have to stay after school to practice. We can rehearse partly during school hours and partly at noon."

"It isn't the practicing," Krissy said, looking away from Mrs. Steele's black hair that shone in the sun like the blackness of magpie feathers. "It's that . . . I don't feel like it." She lowered her eyes. The words on Mrs. Steele's book, open on her desk, were blurred at the edges.

"But I thought you were so glad about it yesterday."

"I was," Krissy admitted. "But that was before it happened. About our dog, I mean. About Skip . . ." She felt her voice tremble, so she left the rest of the explanation hanging there in the air.

"Oh, I'm sorry. There's nothing worse than to have something happen to a dog! What kind was he, Kristine?"

"A border collie," Krissy sort of whispered.

"I never had a collie," Mrs. Steele said. Her voice seemed to come from far away. "But I know how you feel. I had a little mutt dog once, with short legs and the funniest freckled face you ever saw. And ears that seemed to talk a language of their own."

Krissy knew how *that* was. Skip's ears seemed to talk, too.

"I'll never forget how I felt when he was run over," Mrs. Steele went on. "But I just couldn't train him to keep away from cars." She paused. "I wouldn't have felt like playing the Queen of Hearts either, right then. There's something about a dog, isn't there?"

"Oh yes, yes," Krissy cried inside. Even if he didn't get run over. Even if he only went blind. She nodded at Mrs. Steele.

"But, Kristine, you don't have to decide about the part right away. Valentine's Day is more than three weeks off. Why don't you wait till next week? You may feel different about it then."

Krissy shook her head. How could she ever feel different? Knowing what Dad would say?

"Things happen," her teacher said softly. "There's nothing we can do about them, Kristine. Nothing except to carry on the best way we can. Your dog wouldn't want you to give up the part in the play. Would he? But don't decide now when you feel so bad. Tell me a week from today . . . that will be plenty of time."

The gong sounded, and Krissy went to her seat. She didn't even notice that everyone was looking at her, curious to know what she had said to Mrs. Steele.

What was Skip doing? Krissy wondered during arithmetic. Where was Skip now? she wondered during social studies. When would Dad find out? What would he say? What would he do? Dad and Eric would be home from the Stock Show tonight. How long could she keep the secret? Oh, Skip, Skip.

Every once in a while she bent down over her book so no one would notice, and kept her eyes shut, to see what it was like to be blind.

# 4                                Lucky for Eric

KRISSY COULDN'T WAIT to get home from school that afternoon. She wanted to start right away to put maps in Skip's head: where all the barbed-wire fences were, where the sheds and barns were, and the paths, and the old mine holes that prospectors had left when they hunted for gold, years before.

She realized now that Skip's blindness hadn't really come all of a sudden. She kept remembering little things — when she was supposed to be studying, even during singing class. Skip bumping into those dead branches the day he scurried across the gulch after a rabbit. Skip snagging his ear on the fence. Skip not wanting to run for snowballs any more. No, it hadn't come all at once.

The eight miles home in the school bus seemed endless. Sharon never was good at making talk. And Krissy couldn't just sit there worrying about Skip. Verna might notice and wonder what was wrong. So Krissy made herself talk about the catch-it calf contest. "I wonder if Eric caught a calf," she said.

"Is it hard?"

"Well, it's not *easy*, not with twice as many boys trying to catch a calf as there are calves to catch."

"So they don't all get one?"

Sometimes Sharon could ask the dumbest questions. Krissy sighed. How could all the boys get one if there were only half enough!

"I'd like to catch a calf," Sharon mused.

"But even if you could, you couldn't," Krissy told her. "Because you're a girl. You have to be a 4-H Club boy. Besides, you're too young. You have to be at least twelve years old. But most of the boys are usually fifteen and sixteen, Eric says."

They were silent for a moment.

"Anyway," Krissy went on, "it's not easy to get a *chance* to catch a calf. You should see the paper Eric had to sign."

Sharon looked surprised. "What for?"

"He had to agree to all the rules. When he sells his calf at the next Stock Show, he has to give a tenth of the money to the National Western for the Catch-it Calf Fund. But he can keep all the rest, and any prizes he wins. I mean, if he was lucky enough to catch a calf." Krissy looked out the window. They were at the crossroads. Only two more miles and she'd be home with Skip! "Dad had to sign the paper, too," she said. "And the county agent. So you see, it's not easy."

"No, it isn't, is it?"

"But Eric's lucky!" Krissy exclaimed. "He found a half dollar once at the fair grounds."

"I found ten cents," Sharon said. "Right in the middle of the road."

Krissy hopped off the bus, without waiting for Verna. There was Skip, coming up the lane, a little slower than usual. Good old Skip! Good old boy! He didn't *look* blind. "Wait till I change my clothes, Skip," she called.

At first Krisy tried to get him to follow her at the end of a rope. But he didn't like it. He had never been trained to a leash. He kept holding back, pulling against it, walking with his tail between his legs.

He looked so forlorn, Krissy tried a new plan. Perhaps if she sounded cheerful instead of sad, Skip would perk up too. Untying the rope, she gave him a cheery pat. "Come on, boy!" She ran ahead through the thin snow at the side of the barn. Skip trotted after her. He even raised his tail a little. Krissy gave a deep, brave sigh of relief.

And then, just before supper, when Krissy was setting the table, Eric and Dad came honking down the driveway! Honking like two kids, as Mom said. Krissy rushed into her overshoes and coat and ran out to meet them. Would they be bringing home a calf, a catch-it calf?

"Did you catch one, Eric?" was the first thing she called when the car stopped.

It was too dark to see Eric's face, but she knew from the sound of his voice that he was grinning all over. "Look in the back of the truck," he said.

There was the calf! A rumpled-looking Shorthorn calf tied in a makeshift stall, so he wouldn't skid all over the truck.

"Meet Lucky," Eric said, full of eagerness. "That's what I named him, Kris. Lucky! Because I was lucky to get him."

"Lucky!" Krissy gulped. That was what she had said about herself, just yesterday, before she found out about Skip. When she was still the Queen of Hearts. She was glad Eric couldn't see her face.

"Oh, it's big, Eric!" she cried. "I didn't think it would be that big."

"Four hundred and fifteen pounds, and lively as a mule," Eric told her proudly. "He's only grade C, but I bet I can build him up to C plus or maybe even B before I take him back to the show next year. I bet I can make him more than double his weight. I should get a good price for him."

Dad was unloading things, carrying them into the house, shouting to everyone. Skip came and stood near the truck. Eric gave him a pat. Then Krissy eased Skip out of the way before Dad came back. She'd have to train Skip to keep away from cars.

What a commotion at the supper table! Everyone was asking questions about the Stock Show. Was it better than last year? Did more cattlemen from all over the country send in their prize stock? How did it feel trying to catch a scared calf with so many people watching?

Krissy was eager to hear what Dad and Eric had to tell, but she seemed to be hearing two things at once. A wheel kept turning, turning in her head, and every spoke of the wheel stood for one word — Skip. The spokes clicked around and around . . . Skip . . . Skip. . . Skip . . . behind all the talk of the Stock Show.

"Tell us more about Lucky," Mom urged, beaming at Eric.

"There was only one other thirteen-year-old boy in the bunch," Dad said proudly. "Most of them were fifteen or sixteen. Eric was the youngest one to catch a calf." He reached for the gravy boat. "I was afraid he wouldn't get one."

"I almost didn't," Eric said. "You see, there were sixteen boys and only eight calves. I didn't even get a chance at one until another fellow lost his hold. Then I grabbed the calf and hung on for dear life."

"Calf dragged him all over the arena," Dad broke in. "But he hung on. Everyone was shouting and clapping for him. Youngest boy and all."

Eric sighed happily. "I finally got the halter on and led him out by the rope. I felt pretty good about that, leading 415 pounds of calf out by the rope."

The rope. Krissy looked down at her plate. It had been awful trying to lead Skip by the rope. She swallowed hard. How was she going to keep the folks from finding out? If only they'd be so interested in Lucky they'd forget about Skip!

On Saturday morning Dad looked across the breakfast table at Krissy. "Busy this morning?" he asked.

Krissy had planned to spend the morning with Skip, taking him around, getting him used to knowing where things were without seeing them. "Not very busy," she said aloud.

"Want to help me? I could use your two hands."

"Doing what, Dad?"

"Peterson's cut up a lot of dead aspens, with that new attachment for his jeep. Stove-length pieces. I can get a load from him cheap, and we can always use the wood."

"Right," said Mom, passing the raspberry jam. "I like the way aspen burns. It makes a quick, hot fire."

"And if I'm off with you, Dad," Krissy said to herself, "you won't be noticing Skip."

"You could help me load the truck, Krissy, and stack the wood when we get home," Dad was saying.

"Sure, Dad."

Dad glanced in Verna's direction, then back to Krissy. "You'll be better at it than Verna. She'd try to load the truck in a design and stack it in a pattern."

Krissy smiled and Dad gave her a wink.

Mom came to Verna's rescue, like a hen clucking over her chicks without playing favorites. "Verna's making over an old dress for Annie, so she'll be busy enough."

They went off together in the truck, Krissy and Dad. Glancing back, she could see Skip standing in the middle of the drive looking after them. He had to see with his ears now, she thought. He had to see with his nose, and with the pads of his feet. And she was still the only one who knew!

"It's going to be a nice day to get the wood," Krissy remarked. "The sun's so bright."

"And the wood ought to be fairly dry," Dad said. "We haven't had new snow for almost a week."

It was always sort of hard to talk to Dad. Unless he asked questions, Krissy didn't know what to say. But soon Dad had a question.

"You got any ideas about Mom's birthday?"

Krissy was surprised. Mom's birthday wasn't until the twenty-sixth of February, and that was a month away. "Already, Dad?"

"It always takes a while to figure out something she'd like that I can get. You got any ideas, Krissy?"

"I know the dream of her life," Krissy answered slowly. She wanted to add: "And oh, Dad, I know the dream of my life, too. And it isn't anything you'd have to buy. It's only to let me keep Skip, Dad. Only to let me keep Skip!" Aloud she said, "I heard her tell Mrs. Craghorn over the phone."

"Is that so? What is it, Krissy?"

"A bathroom."

"A bathroom!" Dad groaned. "She might as well want the moon, the way things have been going lately. Crag-

horn works in town. He can afford a bathroom; he earns
real money. I put in a lot more time than he does, and
what do I get to show for it?"

"Oh, Mom doesn't think of having it right away."
Krissy didn't want to say anything about the gray hair.
"But couldn't we give it to her in pieces, Dad? Like a
faucet, or a bath mat? If I had enough money, that's
what I'd get her — a bath mat. But I've only got fifty-
seven cents left from Christmas."

"Hold onto it, Krissy," Dad said. "Hold onto your
fifty-seven cents. I might have to borrow it from you
sometime!"

Krissy gave him a look. He was only joking, of course.
But you wouldn't know it from looking at his face. His
mouth was straight, not curved. She wished she could
say: "I know how you feel, Dad, because I've got something to worry about too."

But she didn't say anything, and Dad didn't say anything, and pretty soon they were turning in at the Petersons' gate. Their flock of karakul sheep was grazing near
the fence. Dad stopped to watch them. He'd never had
much faith in those sheep. He thought it was a mistake
not to stick to cows. Krissy could remember hearing him
talk about it to Eric and Mom when Mr. Peterson bought
the sheep two years before. "What does Peterson know
about sheep!"

Krissy thought they were nice. They had long, dark
fur, coarse-looking and shaggy, not like the tightly

packed wool on the white sheep at the county fair. The karakuls stood staring at the truck, their narrow black faces lifted in curiosity. "They look smart, Dad, don't they?" Krissy said. "And I think they're real pretty."

"Hummmp," Dad grunted. "I'm afraid Peterson's going to lose money on them."

"Nothing looks pretty to Dad unless it pays its way," Krissy mused. "Not even something that doesn't belong to him. Mom's different. She looks at things the way I do. Dad has such a funny idea of what's pretty."

Sharon came out to help load the truck, and Mr. Peterson came to talk with Dad. Krissy couldn't help hearing snatches of what they said about the price of beef and feed, about taxes being raised again, about needing new tires. Then Dad asked how the sheep were working out.

"I finally sold last year's fleeces," Mr. Peterson replied. "Held them for months, hoping for a better price. I didn't come out too well. But if I have good luck with the lambs this spring, I'll do all right."

Dad mumbled something Krissy couldn't hear.

"Yes," Mr. Peterson repeated, "if I have good luck with the lambs, I'll be satisfied."

Krissy was to remember that later when the lambs began to disappear.

The day before she had to tell her teacher definitely about the Queen of Hearts, Krissy had a scare. Two scares, in fact.

So far no one had found out about Skip, but Eric was getting close. Several times Krissy had noticed him giving Skip a queer look. Then one day when Eric was bringing in an armload of wood after school, he almost stumbled over Skip. "Can't you get out of the way?" she heard Eric scold. "What's the matter with you?"

Later when Eric went back to the chopping block near the shed, to split some of the aspen pieces into kindling, Skip got in the way again. Eric, swinging the ax for a good crack at the wood, almost hit Skip on the head. Krissy came on the run. "You crazy dog," Eric was scolding. "You're going to get hurt. What's the matter with you, anyway?"

Words made a lump in Krissy's throat. She wanted to say them, but she couldn't. Eric might be like Dad — keeping all those records on Lucky, watching him pay his way. She wanted to cry out that Skip couldn't help getting in the way, because he was blind . . . because he couldn't see a *thing*. Instead she turned quickly away and whistled for Skip to follow. He trotted after her toward the gulch.

# 5                                    Night Alarm

THAT NIGHT IN BED Krissy knew she must make up
her mind about the Valentine play. She still didn't
feel like the Queen of Hearts. She lay there wide awake,
staring at the ceiling, wondering how Annie could sleep
so soundly. She sighed. "I hope I don't dream about Skip
falling downstairs again . . . or about Dad finding out."

She didn't know how long she had been asleep. It was
still black as pitch when she heard Skip barking and barking. The noise seemed to come from out near the corral,
but she couldn't be sure.

What was the matter? Was something after Skip? Or
after Eric's catch-it calf? Or Mom's chickens? Krissy lay
there listening. Should she call Dad?

Just then the door on the other side of the living room
opened, and she heard footsteps creaking across the cold
floor into the kitchen. Dad must be wondering about the
barking, too. If he went out with the flashlight to where
Skip was . . . Krissy jumped out of bed. If Dad flashed the

light on Skip's eyes, he might see the film over them!

In a rush, Krissy got into her clothes. It was hard finding her things in the dark, but she didn't switch on the light for fear of waking Verna.

Picking up her shoes, Krissy tiptoed into the kitchen. She blinked at the sudden brightness of the light. Dad had poked up the coals in the stove, and was putting on his overshoes. He looked up in surprise. "What are you up for, Krissy?" he asked. "It's only four o'clock."

"I heard Skip. You don't think there's anything the matter with him, do you, Dad?"

"*Something's* the matter. I don't know what. Skip doesn't bark that long without some reason. I'm going out to see." He was taking his gun down from its high place over the cupboard.

"I'm going, too, Dad."

"It's cold, Krissy. You better stay by the fire. I can call you if I need you."

"But Dad, if you have to shoot something — a skunk or something — you can't hold the light and shoot too."

"That's right. Well, as long as you're dressed, come along. Button up your collar and put on your overshoes. I just hope this isn't a wild-goose chase. I hope Skip didn't see his shadow and get scared."

"Skip doesn't get scared, Dad," Krissy said. And then to herself: "And he can't see his shadow. He can't see his shadow or anything else. Not any more."

They were going toward the barn, Dad flashing the

light down on the thin new snow. "At least we can be sure it isn't a skunk," he said in a low voice. "They sleep all winter, you know, down at the end of a warm burrow."

Krissy had forgotten.

"Might be a bobcat or a coyote, though. I'll turn out the light and we'll sneak up quietly."

They moved slowly ahead through the darkness. A few stars were out, but they seemed very dim and far away. Skip was still barking, barking, near the corral. Krissy stubbed her toe on a rock and stumbled. She caught at Dad's sleeve. He held her with his free hand, and they moved on quietly, close to each other. Just the two of them there in the great dark hole of night! "Oh, Dad," Krissy thought, "if only you could feel close to Skip too."

"Something at the corral," Dad whispered. "I hope Lucky's all right."

"It's near the little shed," Krissy whispered back. "That's where Skip is."

"We'll creep up quietly." Dad gave Krissy the flashlight. "Here. You flash the light when I give the signal. If you see anything move, try to keep the light on it so I can get a shot."

"You won't hit Skip, will you?" Krissy asked in panic.

"Skip's big enough to take care of himself."

But Dad didn't *know*.

They were getting close to the corral now. Everything looked so different in the dark — the barn, the sheds, the chicken house. They loomed up black against black.

"Now," Dad said. "Flash the light near Skip."

Krissy sent a beam in the direction of the barking. It caught the white of Skip's tail, the tan of his back, the excited upward movement of his head. He seemed to be barking toward the roof of the low shed with one side open to the corral.

"Higher, Krissy."

She ran the beam across the shed roof, stopping at something black hunched at one corner. No eyes showed to catch the light and reflect it. She held the flashlight steady. "See it, Dad?"

"Looks like a porcupine. A big old war horse of a porcupine. I just hope Skip didn't get into it before it crawled up out of reach. Come on, we can get closer if that's all it is."

Krissy flashed the light on Skip, still barking angrily. She didn't see any quills sticking out of his nose. "Thank goodness!" she sighed. If Dad had to get that close to Skip's nose with the tweezers . . .

"Give us some light, Krissy," Dad was saying. "Is Skip all right?"

"Yes. But what about Lucky, Dad? Do you think Lucky would go bunting at a porcupine?" Krissy swung the light around. She remembered how one of the horses had pushed at a porcupine once and come out with a nose full of stinging quills. She remembered what a time Dad and Mr. Peterson and Mom had trying to pull them out.

Lucky was lying on some straw in a corner of the shed. He looked all right. "I'm glad Skip scared the porky to the roof before Lucky got into trouble," Krissy said. She wanted Skip to have the credit. She wanted Dad to see what a good dog he was.

"Well, I'm glad the porcupine got out of the way before *Skip* could reach it," Dad answered. "Dogs haven't much sense when it comes to porkies." He wasn't going to scold Skip for barking, but he wasn't going to praise him either. "The porky probably came around looking for salt."

"Lucky's salt!" Krissy exclaimed. "He came for some of Lucky's salt. And if Lucky caught him licking at it, he *might* have bunted him."

"Could be," Dad conceded.

They heard footsteps running across the yard, heard a voice call out in the darkness. "Is Lucky all right? What's the matter?" What's going on?" It was Eric.

"Just a porcupine," Dad answered. "Skip's got him treed on the shed roof." Then in a lower voice, "See if you can focus the light on his nose, Krissy. I want to get a shot, and his nose is the only place to aim at. You can put a dozen bullets in a porky's hide and not kill him."

The porcupine had its little black forepaws over its face, covering its nose, trying to keep it safe. Krissy wished she were back in bed, away from all this. "But do you have to kill him, Dad?"

"A porky hasn't any business in a barnyard. He doesn't mix well with dogs and calves, Krissy. Any animal that's out of place has to go. Get the light on his nose."

"Any animal that's out of place!" Krissy repeated to herself. "Is a blind dog out of place, Dad? Is he? Is he?"

Eric joined them and Krissy thrust the flashlight at him. "You do it, Eric. I'll get Skip out of the way. Come, Skip." She had to pull him away, pull him into the darkness. He was trembling with anger and excitement over the porcupine.

"There! Hold the light there," Dad was telling Eric.

Krissy knelt in the snow, her arms around Skip's neck. His collar was so thick and deep in winter. He gave a quick movement and kissed Krissy's cheek. Bang! went Dad's gun. Bang!

"I probably got him with the first shot," Dad said. "Just gave him the extra one for good measure. Leave him there on the roof, Eric. I'll bury him in the gully in the morning."

"Oh, Skip," Krissy breathed, her face next to the collie's. "Dad says an animal that's out of place has to go. But *you* aren't out of place. Only how can we prove it to Dad?"

# 6

## Flicker of Hope

GETTING UP SO EARLY because of Skip's barking, Krissy felt she had lived half a day by the time the school bus came. She was at the gate well ahead of time, eager to tell Sharon about all the excitement.

Finally the bus came rattling down the road. Krissy gave Skip a final pat. "Time to go back now, Skip. I'll tell you this afternoon about the Queen of Hearts. I have to let Mrs. Steele know, and I still can't decide." She turned toward the bus. Verna and Eric were hurrying up the lane with their books and lunch boxes.

Sharon always saved a place for Krissy, so they could sit together. "What do you think, Sharon!" Krissy said, the minute she sat down. "I got up at four o'clock this morning."

"You did?"

"It was blacker than velvet. Dad and I went sneaking across the yard." Vividly she told about the adventure with the porcupine. "And Skip didn't get a single quill in his nose," she finished.

Sharon was impressed. "All that at four o'clock in the morning!" Then she said slowly, almost apologetically, "I've got something to tell, too. But it's just funny — not exciting like the porcupine."

"What is it?" Krissy asked.

Sharon unwrapped a newspaper-covered package on her lap and showed Krissy a dozen magazines with bright covers. "Look what my cousin sent me from St. Louis: children's magazines. They're old ones, and she doesn't want them any more, but they're full of stories and poems and things."

Longingly, Krissy turned some of the pages. She hoped Sharon would lend her the magazines, one at a time, to read from cover to cover.

"Here's one called *Story Parade*," Sharon said, "and it's got something real funny about Valentines." She thumbed through the pages awkwardly, looking for the place.

"Why doesn't she hurry?" Krissy thought. "Why is she always so slow?"

"Here," Sharon said at last. "It's a poem. Listen." She began to read in a droning voice:

> I thought I'd buy some gay designs
> For all my friends for Valentines.
> So off I hurried to the shops
> To see what styles were Valentops.

"Valentops!" Krissy exclaimed. "What a fun-word!"

"There's more," Sharon assured her. "That's only the

beginning." She began reading again:

> How red the hearts! How gay the rhymes,
> In keeping with the Valentines.

Krissy smiled. What a nice short way to say it. But it takes her so long to get out the words! She leaned over and read ahead while Sharon's voice mumbled in the background.

> But oh, the prices! I could see
> That I was up a Valentree.

Valentree, Valentree, Krissy said to herself merrily.

> I wish that I could turn a trick,
> I thought. What makes a Valentick?
> The size? The colors front and back?
> I'll try a different Valentack!

Krissy smiled as she read. Oh, they were fun, weren't they, all these Valentricks? And they weren't over yet:

> So giving several silent cheers,
> I wiped away my Valentears
> And hurried home with eager haste
> To illustrate my Valentaste.
> I mixed some dough and rolled it thin
> And baked it in a Valentin,
> But cut it first in shapely hearts —
> For scads and scads of Valentarts.

That made Krissy pause. Because that is what the Queen of Hearts did in the play. She made tarts. Valentine tarts. Valentarts!

> I frosted them with I LOVE YOU,
> Which certainly is Valentrue,
> And all my friends exclaimed, "How *sweet*,
> To think of such a Valentreat!"

Krissy heard herself laughing out loud, the way she used to. She felt the way she liked to feel. Sharon, who was still reading the poem, looked up. "Oh Krissy, you haven't laughed for a week," she exclaimed with relief. "You've been so sort of sad about something. Oh Krissy, I'm glad you can still laugh."

"So am I," Krissy said to herself. "And so will Skip be, too. My being sad doesn't help him see any better."

She turned to Sharon eagerly. "I'm going to make Skip some Valentarts ... in keeping with the Valentimes! And, Sharon, I'm going to play the Queen of Hearts, after all."

She told them at supper that night, after Eric finished talking about Dick Eberhole — Dick Eberhole and the broken glass. "He was racing down the hall with Barry after him," Eric said, "when he pushed on the door and his hand slipped."

"Whose hand?" asked Verna.

"Dick's. His hand slipped and crashed right through the plate glass, and a piece jabbed into his arm. They had to take him to the doctor. He got six stitches!"

"I wonder who'll pay for the glass," Dad mumbled. "The taxpayers?"

"I don't know. But Dick's going to have to wear a sling the rest of the week." Eric sounded envious. "With his right arm in a sling, he won't have to do any writing, or arithmetic, or anything. For the rest of the week — gee!"

"It's a good thing he doesn't have a catch-it calf," Dad said, "or he couldn't take care of it."

"That's right," Eric agreed. And Krissy could see he was glad his arm wasn't in a sling, after all.

"I'm going to be in the play," Krissy said quietly. "The Valentine play. I'm going to be the Queen of Hearts."

"That's wonderful, Krissy!" Mom flashed a happy smile.

"What's the Queen of Hearts?" Annie wanted to know.

"She patches up broken hearts and makes them new again. It's the best part in the play — the longest anyway." Krissy sounded eager, the way she used to sound about things — as if she couldn't *wait* to get started.

"Well, I'm glad you got the part," Verna said. "You've been acting glum lately, Krissy."

Oh, then Verna *had* noticed. Looking through the needles and thread and dress patterns, Verna had noticed.

"Not glum," Mom corrected. "Just quiet and thoughtful, as if you had something on your mind."

"What do you know about the Queen of Hearts?" Dad asked, helping himself to more creamed potatoes. "What do you know about hearts?"

Krissy looked at him. He was busy breaking up his meat ball and mixing it with the potatoes. "Well . . . I just have to say the lines." To herself she finished: "If I only knew about *your* heart, Dad! That's the whole trouble."

The next morning Sharon came running across the pasture as fast as her sturdy legs would carry her. Sharon running! Something must be wrong, Krissy thought, waiting at the door.

Sharon came in, panting. "It's Daisy. She's sick. She's going to have a colt, and she's awful sick."

"Oh, I'm sorry, Sharon," Mom said. "Is there anything we can do? Here, sit down at the table and catch your breath. We're just finishing breakfast."

"Pop wants you to call the vet," Sharon said, flopping into a chair. "Will you?"

Dad was already at the phone, looking up the number. "Did he say which vet he wanted, Sharon?"

Sharon shook her head. "The best, I guess. Daisy's a real good horse."

Dad was dialing. "I'm trying Doc Warren," he said as he waited for an answer. "He's best with horses. Hegner's best with cows."

A vet! Krissy's heart began to thump so hard she could hear it in her ears. Why hadn't she thought of that? Best with horses, best with cows . . . there must be a vet who was best with dogs! Why couldn't a vet find out what was wrong with Skip's eyes? Why couldn't a vet get Skip to see again?

She didn't even hear Dad talking on the phone, she was so excited. Now he turned to Sharon. "He can't come until late this morning."

"My father thinks probably any time before noon ought to be all right," Sharon said. "If he'll be sure to come."

Dad turned back to the phone. "All right, then. And can you plan to stay on into the afternoon if necessary? This is a serious case."

On into the afternoon! Then the vet might still be there when school was out. Krissy grasped at the hope, her heart beating fast.

She'd take Skip and cut through the pasture to Sharon's after school. She'd take all the money she had. Fifty-seven cents wouldn't be enough, but maybe the vet would let her pay the rest on time — like buying a washing machine or a TV set. Would he trust her? When he saw Skip, he would. She'd get the vet to look at Skip's eyes.

Never was a school day longer. The hands of the clock on the wall under the ventilator barely moved. Even reading, which usually went too fast, crawled like a snail. And arithmetic was a hundred snails. And geography a thousand.

And why did the school bus make so many stops?

"What's the matter, Krissy?" Sharon asked. "You're all jumpy."

"Am I?" Krissy tried to hold down the anxiety inside of her, so it wouldn't pop out with her voice.

"You'd think *you* had Daisy and the colt to worry about, 'stead of me. I've been worrying all day, wondering how they are and if the vet got there in time."

Krissy looked at Sharon quickly. Yes, her face was full of worry. And Krissy hadn't even thought of Sharon's being anxious; she'd only thought of Skip. People were all like peas in a pod, weren't they? All closed up in their own pods. "I'm sorry," she said gently. "But you don't have to worry. The vet will know what to do, won't he, Sharon?"

"I hope so," Sharon sighed.

"I'll change my clothes and get Skip and take the short cut over. I want to see the new colt."

"But that isn't all," Krissy thought. "I want the vet to take a look at Skip!"

Sharon felt better, hearing the confidence in Krissy's voice. "I wonder if it'll be a filly," she said. "I wonder if it'll look like Daisy."

Finally Krissy was on her way to the Petersons' ranch with Skip. "It's funny," she told him as they hurried across the pasture, "how things go along for days and weeks without seeming to move. And then all of a sudden things begin to happen fast."

He had been following after her, but now he caught a fresh scent and ran ahead eagerly. That's how Skip had always been — quick and eager and adventurous. Krissy watched as he sniffed excitedly over the ground.

Suddenly in his fearless hurry he bumped into a sharp boulder. He backed up and shook his head, shook it hard. There was blood on his nose.

"Oh, Skip!" Krissy ran to him. "You mustn't go so fast when you can't see." She found a handkerchief and wiped off the blood, and patted his head. "Wait till the vet fixes your eyes. Wait till the vet finds out what's wrong, then you can run all you want."

Skip stood quietly listening, moving his ears, as if he understood. With a pang of pleasure, Krissy saw again how his hair parted in a neat line down his back, just as if someone had combed it that way.

At last they were crawling through the farthest fence, heading for the Petersons' barn. Krissy could see Sharon out in the yard with her two little brothers. They waved and ran to meet her.

"You were right, Krissy," Sharon called out. "The vet knew just what to do. It's the *best* little colt."

The vet knew what to do, knew what to do, Krissy's heart thumped as she ran.

"But it isn't a filly," Sharon called. "It's a he, with a white streak on his nose, like Daisy. And the longest legs!"

Knew what to do, knew what to do . . .

"The vet says they're both going to be all right," Sharon smiled as Krissy reached her.

"Where is he?" Krissy asked. She hadn't seen the vet's car yet.

"In the barn with Daisy. Wait till you see."

"I can't wait till the vet sees Skip," Krissy thought as she hurried along. She felt again for the coin purse in her pocket, to be sure it was still there.

But the vet wasn't in the barn.

"Where is he?" Krissy asked, looking around nervously. "Where's the vet?"

"Oh, I thought you meant the *colt*," Sharon said with a laugh. All the worry was gone from her voice. "The vet left about three o'clock. Our bus must have just missed passing him. Look . . ." she pointed at the colt. "Hasn't he got the longest legs!"

Krissy looked through a mist. The vet was gone. How could she ever get a vet to look at Skip now, without Dad's knowing? The flicker of hope died out. "Yes," Krissy said, trying valiantly to make her voice sound steady. "Colts always have the longest legs, don't they?"

# 7

THE NEXT DAY Eric found out.

Every afternoon when he came home from school he worked with Lucky, leading him and teaching him to follow. Eric would put on the halter, grasp a length of rope, and parade his catch-it calf around the corral. Sitting on the top rail of the pole fence, Krissy liked to watch.

This afternoon Eric was giving Lucky a brushing before putting him through his paces, explaining to Krissy at the same time that the 4-H Club motto didn't apply in Lucky's case. "It's a good motto," he said. *"To Make the Best Better.* But when it comes to Lucky, he was far from the best in the first place."

"You did your best to catch him, though," Krissy answered.

Eric laughed.

"And you're doing your best to make him better. So maybe the motto's all right, after all."

Eric rubbed his calf's nose. "Lucky's losing some of his wildness already. I guess he likes to be brushed. Come on, boy, here we go." Lucky tossed his head a few times, then reluctantly began to follow Eric at the end of the rope.

"Pretty soon I'll have to teach him how to stand," Eric called back to Krissy.

"Doesn't he know how to *stand?*"

"I mean square and straight for a judge at the Stock Show.

Both Krissy and Eric had been so engrossed in the catch-it calf that she'd forgotten about Skip. Now, all of a sudden, there he was darting forward, getting mixed up in Lucky's legs. Skip had squeezed in under the bottom pole of the corral . . .

Lucky lunged and almost pulled the rope from Eric's hand.

"Skip!" Krissy jumped from her perch and made a grab for his thick white collar. "Here, Skip! You don't belong in the corral."

"Hey!" Eric shouted angrily. He almost lost his hold on the rope. "Get that crazy dog out of here, Kris. What's the matter with him?"

"I should have watched him," Krissy said, pulling Skip away. "He didn't mean anything. He was just curious, I guess. He didn't mean to get tangled up with Lucky, Eric."

Eric was flushed and angry. His calf was still bucking

around, trying to get loose. Finally Eric managed to pull him to the fence and tie him. "Got my hands all burned on the rope," he said, rubbing his palms together. "That was a close shave. If Lucky had broken loose, there would have been the dickens to pay."

Krissy, holding Skip, looked up questioningly.

"We learned at Calf Club that you have to be sure your calf never gets loose during the early training period. If he once breaks away, he'll try it every time. Whew!" He kept rubbing his hands. "What's the matter with Skip? He never did a thing like that before."

"He didn't know Lucky was so close, maybe."

"Well, if he didn't know," Eric said, "he must be *blind*. That's all I can say."

It sounded so bare, so hard, put like that. Krissy burst out crying. She couldn't help it. She had held in the tears so many times, for fear someone would notice. Now they just came by themselves. They came burning hot, running down her face. "Don't scold him, Eric," she sobbed. "Don't scold him. He *is* blind."

After she had quieted down, she told Eric all about it. "Nobody else knows," she finished. "It's a secret. Don't tell Dad."

Krissy could see Eric was sorry. He came over and knelt down next to her and Skip and patted Skip's head. "Poor old Skip," he said.

"You won't tell, will you?"

"But Dad's bound to find out, Kris. He's bound to notice sooner or later."

"What'll he do . . . when he does?" Krissy whispered.

"I don't know." Eric kept patting Skip's head, keeping his eyes down. "I'm afraid he'll think a blind dog isn't much good."

"Oh, Eric!" It was what Krissy was afraid of, too. For a moment she couldn't say anything. Then . . . "Did you ever close your eyes tight and try walking around without seeing, Eric? It's awful. I've been trying it. That's the kind of world Skip lives in now. And it isn't his fault! He didn't *do* anything."

"I know," Eric said. "It isn't his fault. And I won't tell if you say so. But gosh, Kris, Dad is sure to find out."

"There's the vet." Eagerly Krissy poured out her plan. "I'm going to try to get enough money for the vet." Her eyes shone as if she were acting out a part in a play. "So when Dad finds out, I can say: 'Let's take him to the vet, Dad. He can fix Skip, the way he fixes horses and cows. If you'll just take Skip in the truck, I'll pay. I've got the money.' Isn't that a good idea, Eric? How much do you think it will cost?"

Eric thought it would cost about two and a half dollars for an office call. That sounded like a lot of money.

"Well, fifty-seven cents is a start," Krissy told herself, as she held Skip outside the corral and Eric went back to training his calf. "If it comes to the worst, maybe I can borrow some from Verna. I can't ask Dad. I can't ask

Mom, when she's saving for the bathroom. And I can't ask Eric because he has to buy feed for Lucky."

Yes, Verna was the one to ask. She had been doing some sewing for Mrs. Peterson. And maybe she even had some of the prize money from the county fair last fall. She had won first prize in clothing and second in style review. "I won't ask her yet, though," Krissy decided. "It's still a secret."

Verna came home all excited late that afternoon. She had been at a meeting of the 4-H Sewing Club. "We're going to have a square dance group!" she exclaimed. "And I'm the one chosen to design the dresses. I can just see how they should look — old-fashioned, with full, shirred skirts. I'll make up my dress first for the others to see."

"Good for you, Verna," Mom said. She was proud of the way Verna could sew. "Verna can make something out of nothing," Krissy had heard Mom tell Mrs. Craghorn on the phone. "And she can make something even better out of something!"

"I'll need yards and yards of material," Verna said, her eyes full of plans. "I wish Mrs. Peterson would pay me for the sewing I did for her."

"She hasn't forgotten," Mom hastened to say. "She mentioned it when I saw her the other day. Said she hoped you wouldn't mind waiting a bit. They've had extra expenses lately — the vet, and new tires for the jeep, and Sharon needing a new pair of shoes."

"But I need the money *now*," Verna said, tossing her head. "I've got to get started on my dress. We want to practice in them as soon as we can. I thought I'd sort of look around for material after school tomorrow and ride home with Mr. Craghorn." She turned to Mom appealingly. "Haven't you some egg money put away you could lend me, Mom?"

"But it's for the *bathroom*," Krissy blurted out. "You can't use the bathroom money."

Verna gave her a look.

"I'm afraid it isn't even for the bathroom this month," Mom said. "I have to be thinking about sending for some baby chicks. I've been hoping I could order just pullets this time, and they're much more expensive than pullets and cocks mixed. I don't know how I'm going to make out."

"You see, it isn't for the bathroom!" Verna said sharply to Krissy. Then she changed her tone of voice, sprinkled it with sugar. "You've got some money left from Christmas, Krissy. Haven't you?"

"But I can't lend it to you, Verna," Krissy cried. "I need it."

"What do you need it for?" Verna demanded.

"I can't tell you. But I need it, Verna. I need it even more than you do. Maybe Eric can lend you some."

Verna's voice was shrill. "What do *you* need money for, I'd like to know. You're just making that up. There aren't any birthdays . . . not until Mom's comes, and that's almost a month away. I can pay you back by then."

"But I can't wait that long," Krissy gasped. Oh, it would be wonderful if she could wait, if Dad wouldn't find out right away. But almost a month! It was too much to expect. She shook her head.

"You're just an old meanie, Krissy, that's what you are. A stubborn, selfish, stingy old meanie." With that Verna flounced into the bedroom.

Krissy stood there stunned, looking after her. Beyond the ringing in her ears, she heard Mom's voice. "Don't mind Verna, Krissy. She's just so intent on her sewing, she's upset. *I* know what you're like, and you're not a bit selfish or stingy. You're my . . . my Queen of Hearts. That's what you are."

"Oh Mom," Krissy cried, leaning against her, feeling her arms in a quick hug. If only she could say the rest out loud: "Skip's more important than any old square dance, isn't he?"

# 8                                   That Fool Dog

For SEVERAL DAYS, Krissy and Eric shared the secret,
feeling very close to each other and to Skip — a new
kind of closeness.

"Skip's getting good," she told Eric after a run to
the gulch. "He doesn't bump into things nearly so much.
And he's more sure of himself. He's smart, Skip is."

Eric nodded. "He's smart, all right."

Krissy wished she could do something for Eric, because he was on her side. He wanted Skip even though
he was blind. She wished she could help keep the records
on Lucky, or weigh out his food, or wash him and curl
his hair — anything to show how she felt.

"Lucky's been better ever since I burned my hands
on the rope," Eric said. "Maybe it's a good thing Skip
got mixed up with him, after all. Lucky knows who's
boss around here now. He knows I'm not going to let
go of the rope whatever happens."

And then came the day when Dad almost ran over

Skip with the truck. Krissy was in school. She had tried
to train Skip to keep away from cars, but that was the
hardest thing to do. He was always so quick. And how
could Skip know when a car was going to turn or where
it would go?

Dad talked about what happened at the supper table.
Krissy would never forget. They had lemon pie for des-
sert — her favorite. But she couldn't eat a bite.

"Looks as if we're going to have to get a new dog,"
Dad said. He said it the way he might say, "Looks as
if we're going to have to get a new shovel." As if Skip
were a *thing!*

"I almost ran over Skip with the truck this morning,"
Dad went on, buttering a biscuit. "Might have killed
him."

Krissy trembled. She looked across the table at Eric.
He had his eyes on Dad.

"And the other day I almost broke my neck because
of that fool dog," Dad went on. "I was carrying a bunch
of poles to fix the corral. Skip got right in front of me.
It was a case of swerving quick with the poles or bumping Skip on the head. I slipped and sat down with the
poles all over me. And it wasn't funny!"

"What's the matter with Skip?" Verna asked. "Acting
like that."

"He's gone *blind*. That's what's the matter," Dad
answered.

"Blind? Why, poor Skip!" Mom exclaimed. "I can't believe it. Are you sure? He always knows where to find his supper! Why, poor Skip."

"What's blind?" asked little Carl.

"It means he can't see," Krissy choked, and put down her fork and reached for her handkerchief.

Dad gave her a quick look. "How long have you known, Krissy?"

"Since . . . since you and Eric went to the Stock Show."

"Why didn't you say something?"

"I was afraid." Krissy caught her breath and plunged ahead. She couldn't let herself cry now. She had to speak up for Skip. "But Dad, Skip didn't do anything bad."

"I can't see that a blind dog is much *good*," Dad answered.

"I don't know about that," Mom said, glancing at Krissy.

Krissy looked back at her, wide-eyed and hopeful.

"I hadn't even noticed about Skip," Mom was saying. "He still barks the minute a car stops at the gate, before anyone even opens it. He always warns me in time to take off my apron and fix my hair."

"Oh, Mom!" Krissy thought. "Thanks for telling Dad. Thanks for taking Skip's part."

"Sure," Eric said. "He's still a good watchdog. There's nothing wrong with his ears. They'll probably get even better now."

"What about the cows?" Dad asked. "I've got to pas-

ture them here a couple months of the year. A blind
dog wouldn't be any good keeping them off the windbreak and the shrubbery, to say nothing of your mother's
flower beds. Besides, he's liable to get hurt, with cars
coming in and out."

"Dad," Krissy begged, "can't we take him to the vet?
The vet saved Daisy for the Petersons. And he cured
your sick cow last fall. He'll know what to do for Skip.
And you won't have to pay for it, Dad, because I will.
I've been saving my money."

"Oh!" Verna choked, and reached for her water glass.
"Saving for *that*."

"I doubt if the vet can do anything," Dad said. "Doubt
it very much." He saw Krissy pushing aside her piece of
lemon pie. "Well . . . we can try, Krissy. We can take
Skip down to the vet on Saturday morning."

"Oh Skip, Skip!" Krissy got up from the table and
dashed out the door.

Now that the family knew, Krissy told Sharon on the
way to school next morning.

"Blind!" Sharon exclaimed. "Skip? That's awful, isn't
it?"

"But we're taking him to the vet," Krissy cried, her
voice full of hope. "You know what the vet did for Daisy.
That's what vets are for, isn't it?"

"My father had a blind horse once," Sharon said slowly.
"He said it got along all right. But then, you *drive* a
horse."

"Skip's going to get along all right, too." Krissy was confident. "But I'm going to have to pay the vet on the installment plan, like a washing machine. Fifty-seven cents down. Do you think he'll let me?"

"I can lend you a quarter," Sharon offered. "It's all I've got. But I know how I'd feel if it was Trigger."

"Oh, Sharon!" Krissy flushed. Sometimes she was impatient with Sharon for being so slow and sort of plodding. But then again Sharon was strong and dependable, like mountains and bread. "Thanks, Sharon. I'll do something for you sometime."

Yes, a quarter would help. But if only something bigger would happen, Krissy thought, looking out at the fence posts hopping past the bus window. If only it would rain pennies and dimes . . . If only it would snow quarters and dollars!

"When are you taking him?" Sharon asked.

"Saturday. First chance we can. Dad and I will take him down in the truck. Oh, I can't wait, Sharon. There must be some medicine . . . to help eyes."

"Maybe something will happen before Saturday," Sharon said hopefully, "so you'll get the rest of the money in time. You never know."

"You never know what's going to happen until it happens," Krissy caught herself repeating, "and then it's too late . . ." She stopped. But must it always be too late? Couldn't it, just for once, be in time?

# 9    An Unexpected Move

Eric had a 4-H Club meeting after school and had arranged to ride home with Mr. Craghorn. It was suppertime before Eric finally came rushing into the kitchen. He had stopped only long enough to feed Lucky. "Guess what!" he cried.

"What?" everyone asked.

"We're going to lose a neighbor."

"Who? Who?"

Krissy looked at Eric in fright. There was one neighbor she dreaded losing more than any other. What would she do without Sharon? "The Petersons?" she asked.

"Not the Petersons," Eric answered. "Guess again."

"Well, it can't be the Craghorns," Mom said, "because they're having their well deepened next week while the water is so low. They plan to start building the bathroom as soon as the weather is more certain. I was talking with Grace on the phone today. Imagine, having a bathroom!"

Dad guessed, and Verna guessed, and Krissy guessed

65

again, till there weren't any neighbors left. "Come on, Eric," Mom urged. "You've put us off long enough. Who's going to move?"

"The Craghorns!" answered Eric, wiping his hands on the roller towel.

"The Craghorns!" Mom couldn't believe it. "You must be wrong, Eric. Grace would have told me."

"And what about the *bathroom*?" Krissy asked.

"Mr. Craghorn told me on the way home," Eric explained. "He just found out. Mrs. Craghorn doesn't even know yet." He glanced at the clock on the shelf above the stove. "Well, maybe she's finding out now."

"The Craghorns!" Mom exclaimed again.

"They've had their ranch up for sale for a long time, I understand," Dad said. "But they gave up ever selling it for the price they wanted."

"The real estate company got a buyer this afternoon. Called Mr. Craghorn about four o'clock. He was some surprised," Eric said. "The buyer wants to take possession in two weeks. He's from the East. Doesn't plan to farm, justs wants to live in the country and raise horses. Arabians."

"He must be awful rich," said Krissy.

"Must be," nodded Dad.

"So Mrs. Craghorn won't get her bathroom, after all," Krissy sighed.

"She'll get it a lot sooner than she thought," Verna corrected. "They'll move to town, so she'll get it right away." She turned to Mom. "Maybe she'll give you all the bathroom clippings she collected. Why don't you ask her?"

Mom sighed. "I'll miss Grace. It's the last thing in the world I thought would happen, the Craghorns moving . . ."

After supper, the phone rang. It was for Eric.

"Sh!" Mom told Annie and Carl, who were playing catch-it calf around the living-room table.

Krissy kept looking at the children's magazines Sharon had lent her, but her ears were on the phone. If it was one of those 4-H boys, she could go back to her story . . .

"Yes, sir," Eric was saying.

So it wasn't one of the boys. Who, then?

"Saturday? This coming Saturday. Well, yes, Mrs. Craghorn, I think I can. I'll have to ask Dad though." Eric turned from the phone. "Dad, Mr. Craghorn wants me to work for him Saturday. Is it all right?"

"Far as I know," Dad said.

"Yes, I can do it," Eric said into the phone. There was a pause. Then, "I'm sure my sister Krissy would be glad to help."

"Not Saturday, Eric! Not Saturday," Krissy gasped. "Dad and I are taking Skip to the vet on Saturday. Remember? Can't we do the work next week instead?"

Eric was shaking his head. "Wait a minute," he said to Mr. Craghorn. "Krissy's saying something." He turned, and held his hand over the mouthpiece. "It's got to be *this*

Saturday, Kris. Mr. Craghorn wants the junk carted away from that old tool shed. He wants the shed cleared out."

"But the vet . . ." Krissy cried.

"The vet won't run away," Dad put in. "And Skip is blind already. You'd better take the work when you can get it, Krissy. We can take Skip down to the vet the next Saturday."

But that will be the middle of the month, Krissy thought. The day after the school play. And she'd hoped, oh, how she'd hoped, that the vet would say he could cure Skip *before* she played the Queen of Hearts.

"What do you say, Kris?" Eric was waiting to tell Mr. Craghorn. "You can use the money, can't you?"

Money! Dimes from heaven! What if they had to put off taking Skip? One more week couldn't hurt, could it? "I'll help," Krissy said eagerly. "Tell him I'll be glad to help, Eric."

Eric said that he and Krissy would stop after school to look over the job, and that they would come for sure on Saturday, no matter what the weather. "I figure we can carry junk to the nearest gully, even if it's snowing," Eric told Krissy after he hung up.

"What's he going to pay you?" Dad wanted to know.

"Oh, he's not going to *pay us* exactly . . ."

Krissy's jaw dropped. Not pay? But Eric had said something about money. What did he mean?

"There's a lot of stuff there," Eric explained. "Mr. Craghorn says we can sell the scrap iron down at the junk yard and keep the money, providing we cart all the trash away. He wants the place cleaned up slick as a whistle before he moves."

Dad grunted. "All I can say is you and Krissy had better start before daylight if you're going to cart away all *that* trash."

"What a job," Verna sniffed, "for a little old scrap iron! What a dirty job."

After school, Krissy and Eric rode on past the ranch gate and had the bus driver let them off at the Craghorns' gate. The bus wasn't used to stopping there because there weren't any children at the Craghorns'.

Mrs. Craghorn took them out to the shed and showed them just what had to be done. "My goodness!" she apologized, "I didn't realize there was so much. My husband never likes to throw anything away, and I guess the folks who lived here before didn't either." She shook her head. "I don't see how the two of you can do it without help."

Krissy didn't either.

"Mr. Craghorn wants all the trash carried to that old mine hole at the end of the field, where it will be out of the way and fill up the hole at the same time."

Eric and Krissy looked from the shed to the mine hole. It was a long way to carry things.

"What about that broken-down mowing machine?" Eric asked. "And that old hay rake? And those broken wheels and axle hubs?"

"Everything has to go," Mrs. Craghorn answered. "We want to leave the place neat and clean. After all, we're getting a good price for it, and nobody likes to move in with somebody else's old junk."

"We'll have to get Dad to help with the truck," Eric said. "We couldn't possibly finish otherwise, just the two of us."

Mrs. Craghorn opened the sagging door to the shed. "Then there's all this." She gave a little laugh. "I can't imagine why we saved all those tin coffee cans and glass jars. And rusty nails. Aren't people funny!"

"Verna saves buttons," Krissy said. "But they don't take much room."

"Buttons?" Mrs. Craghorn looked around. "There's a box of old clothes in here somewhere. I was going to cut them up for rags, but I never got around to it. There may be some nice old buttons — you can see when you dig down to them. Anything you want you can have, of course. We're going to move to a much smaller place in town, and just can't take any of this old stuff along. Well, look around. Maybe you have time to separate some of the things now. Stop at the house when you leave. I have a big envelope of pictures and clippings about bathrooms for your mother."

After Mrs. Craghorn left, Krissy and Eric took stock of the old iron they could salvage and sell for scrap. There wasn't too much, they decided, compared to all the trash. "Looks as if we got into something, Kris," Eric said. "This is going to be a lot of work. And I don't know if some of the iron is worth hauling to town."

Krissy gave a little shiver. It was a raw, gray, February afternoon with a bite to the wind. She wished she had on her jeans instead of her school dress flapping around her knees. "Tomorrow's Wednesday," she said. "We could sort out things after school the rest of the week. Then if Dad will help with the truck Saturday morning, and take the scrap iron with him when he goes to town in the afternoon, we ought to be able to finish."

"Maybe," Eric said doubtfully. His eye lit on something lying on one of the discarded chairs. "Look at that, will you?"

"What?"

"That old coffee mill."

"What's it for, Eric?"

"Folks used to grind coffee in them." He picked up the grinder and began to turn the handle. "It still works. What do you know? They used to go to a lot of trouble grinding coffee."

"Is it any good?"

"Sure, it's good. But I don't know what for!" He looked around the shed. "That's the trouble with most of this stuff."

"I just hope the junkman thinks the old iron is good," Krissy said. "Good and valuable."

They talked about the Craghorns' junk at the supper table that night. Eric tried to get Dad interested in helping. "There's some wonderful hardwood in those old wagon wheels, Dad. And I bet if we took the mowing machine apart you could use some of it for spare parts. The hay rake, too."

"No doubt of it," Dad said.

"We saw some other iron pieces that might come in handy on the ranch," Eric went on.

"Oh, Eric, not the iron!" Krissy could hardly keep from blurting out. "Don't talk so much about the iron. We have to sell it to the junkman!"

"Any old axle hubs?" Dad asked. "They're good to set a gate in, so it'll swing easy."

"Sure, Dad." Eric looked across at Krissy. "Krissy and I will be willing to give up anything you can use, if you'll help us Saturday morning. Mr. Craghorn wants the trash thrown in an old mine hole, and it's long way to walk. But it'd be nothing with the truck."

"Can't do it Saturday," Dad said. "Not Saturday morning. When I saw I wouldn't be taking Skip to the vet, I promised John Maxwell I'd help with that loading chute for his cows. He's got the poles all ready and everything. Wants to get the job started . . ."

"But, Dad," Eric pleaded, "we can't possibly do that job for Mr. Craghorn without a truck. And I promised."

"Sorry," Dad said. "I promised, too. John Maxwell's depending on me."

Krissy knew how Eric felt, because she felt the same

way. Sort of hollow inside. All that junk! All that way to the mine hole, and no truck!

Mom spoke up. "I can drive the truck." She looked at Dad. "Why don't I drive you to the Maxwells' first thing Saturday morning, and then help the children? I can arrange my work. And I'd be glad to help. Grace Craghorn is all upset, worrying about getting the place ready on such short notice."

"Oh Mom," Krissy thought, "do it, do it!" She stole a look at Dad. "Let her do it, Dad," she begged inside. "Let Mom drive the truck!"

"I'll help too," Annie offered.

"Me too," said Carl.

"Of all things!" Verna sniffed. "Junk!"

"What about it, Dad?" Eric asked, his voice eager. "We'd save out everything that would come in handy on the ranch."

"Suits me," Dad said. "Don't forget those hubs."

Krissy was so glad she felt like laughing and shouting. Oh, it would be fun, with Mom driving the truck! "It's too bad you don't save *buttons,* Dad — like Verna," she said gaily. "Because we could get you some nice old-fashioned buttons."

"Buttons?" Verna looked interested for the first time.

"Mrs. Craghorn says there's a box of old clothes in the shed that might have some interesting buttons," Eric put in. "Too bad you turn up your nose at junk, Verna."

"Save them for me, Krissy. Save the buttons for me," Verna begged.

"But I'll be awfully busy, and it takes time to cut off buttons. You can't imagine how much stuff there is, Verna. Coffee grinders and everything."

"Coffee grinders!" Verna sat up straight in her chair. There were dreams in her eyes. "Why don't I help, too? Why don't we all help? Maybe I can think of something that's worth more than scrap iron. After all, I keep up on things!"

"You mean you really want to help?" Eric exclaimed.

"Yes, I really do."

Krissy gasped. Imagine, Verna helping with the junk! Well. You certainly never did know what was going to happen.

# 10    Christmas in February

SATURDAY MORNING was clear and bright and not too cold. The ground was frozen hard and almost free of snow, except for a dingy drift here and there. Of course, the north slopes were still white beneath the pines, but there wouldn't be any hills to climb. Krissy couldn't have ordered a better morning if she had thought it all out and written it down.

What a hustle and bustle around the house! Everyone was excited. Everyone except Dad. "You'd think you were going on a picnic, or to the circus or something," he said.

"We are," Mom laughed. "We're going to a three-ring junk circus."

"We'll bring you something for a souvenir, Dad," Eric promised.

"Buttons!" Verna exclaimed. "Oh, I mustn't forget to take the scissors." She ran to the other room.

Krissy slipped outside to tell Skip. He was making the rounds of the yard, the way he did every morning, sniffing and sniffing. Even if he couldn't see, Skip kept up on what was happening around the yard. "You'll have to stay home, Skip," Krissy told him. "Stay home and take care of the house. But all the work I do this morning is for you. And I'm so *glad* to have the chance. Wait till next Saturday. That will be your day, Skip . . . when we take you to the vet, when he gives you some medicine for your eyes."

They all went off together in the truck: Mom and Dad and Verna in the cab; Krissy, Eric, Annie, and Carl in the back, with blankets over them and under them. Eric remembered to take some tools, and Mom had a Thermos jug of hot cocoa and a box of graham crackers. It *was* like a picnic, a picnic in February, Krissy thought.

After they dropped Dad at the Maxwells', they had to double back on their tracks. But by eight o'clock they were ready to get to work. Oh, but it wasn't work, Krissy told herself gaily. It wasn't work to do something for Skip, with all of them there together.

Annie and Carl peeked into the shed, and soon there was a shriek of delight. "Lookit what I found!" Annie came out with a doll buggy. Only three wheels were good, the fourth was mostly wobble, and the stuffing bulged from the seat. But Annie's eyes glistened with more than sunlight. "It's like *Christmas*," she shouted.

"Kissmus, Kissmus," echoed Carl, striking the ground with a broken-handled hoe.

Yes, it was. Krissy smiled. It was like having Christmas all over again. Christmas in February! She saw the end of a pipe wedged under a box bulging with old magazines, and pulled it out. "Oh, Mom," she called. "Here's even a piece of pipe for your bathroom."

Mom laughed merrily. "Put it on the pile of things to take home, Krissy."

Verna was all excited when she found an old kerosene lamp with a brass base and a tall, dirty chimney. "If only there were a pair of them," she sighed. "If only I could find another. Help me look, Krissy."

"What for? Nobody uses kerosene lamps any more."

"Oh, *don't* they," Verna answered mysteriously.

"Kissmus! Kissmus!"

"Say it again, Carlie," Annie giggled, abandoning the doll buggy for a moment to give him a quick hug.

"Hey, Krissy . . ." Eric was calling as he tugged at an old, round, high living-room stove with tarnished nickel trim. "Give me a hand with this stove. There's a lot of scrap iron in it."

"Take out the grates first," Mom suggested. "Then it won't be so heavy."

Everyone was excited. Krissy saw Mom poking around, eager as a kid. Today they were all in the same pod, weren't they? All except Dad and Skip. Today they were six in a pod, instead of only one or two. It gave her a warm feeling. She unbuttoned the top button of her jacket and ran to help Eric with the stove.

Back and forth to the truck they went, their arms piled high with junk. Finally Eric and Mom drove off to the mine hole with a jiggly load. Then back and forth, loading the truck again. And Annie parading around in an old silk dress without any buttons, because Verna had the buttons in her pocket. And Carl trying to screw rusty nuts on rusty bolts. And Mom wondering if Dad could use the wheel of an old grindstone. Oh, it was fun!

Eric promised to give Annie and Carl a dime apiece for helping. "And we'll have to figure out how to split the rest of the money," he said.

"Split it four ways," Verna answered pertly. "We're all helping, you and Mom and Krissy and I."

"But that's hardly fair, Verna," Mom objected. "Eric and Krissy have been working here after school, taking things apart and salvaging the wood and all."

"You're driving the truck, Mom," Eric pointed out. "We couldn't get along without the truck."

"And *I*," said Verna, "I have an idea that might bring as much money as the scrap iron." She tossed her head grandly. "I think splitting the money four ways is fair enough."

What was Verna's idea? Krissy wondered. Did it have something to do with needles and thread and buttons?

The morning had wings. "And so have we," Krissy thought, as she hurried to the truck with her umpteenth box of old cans. "We're like a little flock of birds, scratching around. Six birds, all different sizes, and full of chirps."

And then at the back of a shelf in the shed, Krissy found something she had wanted all her life!

At first she couldn't believe it. Was it really real, under its layers of dust and grime?

Carefully she reached for the little china teapot. She had yearned for just such a teapot to go with her set of dishes. The painted tin one she had didn't belong. It was cheap-looking and gaudy, and no fun to use.

Breathlessly, Krissy wiped off her find. The cover was in place and not even chipped on the outside. The nick inside the neck didn't matter. The golden knob on the cover was faded, but you could still tell it was gold. And there were still sprigs of pink roses on each side of the pot. The spout was chipped, but surely it would pour.

"Here's something I'm going to keep for myself," Krissy cried, showing off her treasure. "Isn't it wonderful?"

"For what?" asked Eric.

"And only the spout nicked!" Mom exclaimed.

"Too small to be much good," said Verna appraisingly.

"For *tea* parties?" Annie asked, envy trembling in her voice.

"Yes, for tea parties. But I'm the only one who's to pour, Annie," Krissy said. "I'll invite you and Carl to a tea party, but you're not to touch it, because it's so *special*."

Talk about Christmas. Christmas in February!

With great care, Krissy wrapped the little teapot in newspapers and packed it in a cardboard box and tied it round and round with a piece of binder twine. She put the box near the pile of things they were saving to take home. Wait till she showed Sharon! Wait till she had Sharon over for a tea party!

By noon, all the trash was in the mine hole and the truck was loaded with scrap iron to be taken to town. Scrap iron and Verna's big box! "I'm keeping these things separate," Verna kept saying all morning, whenever she found something that gave her an idea.

"What for?" Eric asked.

"You take care of selling the scrap, Eric. And I'll take care of disposing of these. We'll split four ways on everything." That was all Verna would answer.

Krissy couldn't understand why Verna wanted some of those old things. Three kerosene lamps. An old vinegar jug. The coffee mill. A dented brass kettle. The spout section of a rusty little pitcher pump. Some big pictures in tarnished frames. Old glassware, some of it colored orange and pink, and full of "warts."

Verna packed her selections carefully in a big box, and what a time Eric, Verna, and Mom had getting it up on the truck! "Tie it on," Verna insisted. "I don't want anything to jiggle and break."

But who'd pay money for any of those things? Krissy kept wondering. Who'd want kerosene lamps when electricity was easier? Or a hand coffee grinder?

"Dad will have to come get *our* things later," Mom said. She looked around. Her cheeks were rosy and her eyes sparkly and her hair wisping out from under one of

Eric's caps. "It was fun, wasn't it?"

Krissy, Eric, and Verna had to walk home because there wasn't room to ride. Krissy carried her teapot. She wasn't going to take a chance on leaving it. Verna had a can that rattled with buttons, like Halloween. Eric had his pockets full of odds and ends, and a strap with a big brass buckle around his waist. He tried to get Verna to tell what she was going to do with the box, but she put him off. "You and Dad and I will take the stuff down later this afternoon," she said. "You'll both have to help unload the box where I want it. I'll split with you later."

Krissy had things all figured out. If her share of the junk money amounted to $1.43, she'd have two dollars for the vet, without borrowing Sharon's quarter. Was that too much to expect? She had worked it all out with a stick, making the figures in the hard earth. If her share was to be $1.43, they'd have to get $5.72 for the junk. Surely a load of old iron ought to be worth *that* much.

The morning had flown like a bird, but the afternoon crawled like a snail. Krissy played with Skip and took him for a walk and helped Mom clean the house. She washed the little teapot, and kept running to her shelf in the bedroom to admire it. She scraped carrots for supper and set the table. And still the truck didn't come back from town.

But finally headlights came flashing down the lane. Krissy rushed out, with Mom's old coat over her head and shoulders. Verna's box was gone. The truck was empty except for feed sacks and a box of groceries. And there was Eric getting out. "Did you sell it? Did you sell it?" Krissy cried.

"You bet," Eric answered. "And the junkman gave me *ten dollars*, Kris. That's two-fifty apiece. Pretty good, don't you think?"

Two-fifty apiece! Krissy's heart leaped. Then even if the vet charged three dollars, she'd have enough to pay him in full! And the teapot besides. And all the other things they'd saved to take home. Why, in a way it was even *better* than Christmas.

Verna hurried into the house with her packages, and Krissy threw her arms around Eric, almost losing Mom's coat. "Ten dollars is wonderful, isn't it? Oh, Eric, I didn't know if the vet would want to be paid like a washing machine!"

Eric laughed and began to unload the groceries.

"There's still Verna's money," he said.

"You mean Verna's is extra?"

"Sure. What she got for her box. But she won't tell. Not till suppertime, she says."

"You mean we'll each get more than two-fifty?" Krissy couldn't believe it.

"She must have sold something," Eric answered. "Because she came home with some packages. Said she found just the right material for her square dance dress."

Verna was like that, not wanting to tell right away, making everyone wonder and wait. Like a movie. Like the exciting part of a book. "And there's no use asking her," Krissy sighed. "She won't tell until she gets good and ready."

Verna wasn't ready to tell until Mom began dishing up the tapioca pudding. Then she started with the square dance material, opening the end of a brown-paper package and passing it around. "Look. Isn't it pretty? It was worth waiting for."

"Lovely," Mom said. "But that's not a cheap material, Verna."

"No, it isn't. But for once I didn't have to spend anything for buttons! I'm going to use some of those old-fashioned Craghorn buttons. They'll give just the right touch."

"Did you *pay* for it?" Krissy asked, admiring the goods.

"Of course, I paid for it."

"Aw, come on, Verna, don't keep us in suspense," Eric urged. "If you don't hurry, I'll tell where you had us unload the box."

"Let me tell!" Verna said sharply. "In my own way, please."

"Get along with you," Dad interrupted. "I drove the truck and wrestled with that box. *I'll tell.*" He looked at Mom. "Where do you think that daughter of ours took that box?"

"I can't imagine."

"To the antique shop!"

"Antique shop?" Mom exclaimed. "Really, Verna?"

"I've a notion not to tell now," Verna pouted.

"Come on," Dad urged. "Nobody knows how you made out; if you got ten cents for the stuff or twenty. You've got us all guessing."

That made Verna feel better, to keep folks guessing. "Yes, I went to the antique shop," she said, "even though Dad told me it was a crazy idea. And I put on a demonstration."

"A demonstration?" Mom asked. "What do you mean?"

"Of the *junk?*" Krissy exclaimed, forgetting to eat her pudding. "A demonstration of the junk?"

"Of the *antiques,*" Verna corrected. "You remember those kerosene lamps? Well, I showed the man how easily they could be wired for electricity, and how modern they'd look with plaid lampshades. I drew him a picture. And that section of pitcher pump will make a most unusual planter. I sketched that out, too."

"What's a planter?" asked Eric. "If it doesn't plant corn or grain?"

"Why, it's a holder for plants and vines, silly. Can't you just see a vine trailing down that spout?"

"I'll be switched," said Dad.

"I had ideas for everything," Verna went on. "The coffee mill can be either a planter or a lamp. And some of the little doodads will make unusual knobs for drawers. And the picture frames . . . artists are always looking for old picture frames." She shrugged and tossed her head. "I sold everything."

"But how did you *know*, Verna? Where did you get all those ideas? I didn't think anyone would want warty glasses." Krissy looked across the table in admiration. "How did you think of it all?"

"It's what I like to do," Verna answered. "I keep up on things. Let's see." She reached for her purse. "What's twelve divided by four?"

"Twelve what?" Eric asked excitedly.

"Dollars." Verna said it as calmly as if money grew on fence posts. "I sold the whole lot for twelve dollars. I could have got a lot more, but when the owner offered me a job Saturday afternoons, I let it go for twelve."

"A job!" Mom exclaimed. "What kind of job?"

"Helping with lamp shades and ideas."

"Oh, Verna," Krissy thought, looking at her sister wide-eyed. "And I thought all you had in your head was needles and thread!"

"That's three dollars apiece," Eric cried. "Gosh! With the scrap-iron money, that'll buy a lot of feed for Lucky."

"And I can get the baby chicks," Mom said happily. "I can get the little pullets without even making a dent in the bathroom!"

Krissy's eyes were glistening. "And I can take Skip *twice*. So if the vet doesn't fix his eyes the first time, I can take him again. And buy some medicine, too. Oh, it's like Christmas and Thanksgiving all rolled together with ice cream on top!"

# 11          At the Vet's

THE NEXT FRIDAY was Valentine's Day, and Krissy was bubbling over like a meadow lark. Verna had actually *offered* to let the Queen of Hearts wear the red skirt, and had even sewn some gold braid on it and gathered it at the waist so it would fit. And Mom had helped Krissy sew red hearts on her blouse. And Eric had studded the gold paper crown with rivets, so it looked very fancy.

Krissy packed her costume carefully in an old suit box. In addition she took a small cardboard box to school with her that morning.

"What's in the little box?" Sharon asked. "Your crown?"

Krissy smiled teasingly. "A secret."

"Valentines?"

"I told you I wasn't going to *send* any Valentines this year, Sharon."

"I know. But I can't believe it. Because everybody sends Valentines."

All week Sharon had been working on Valentines —

cutting, pasting, printing, trying to think of rhymes. All week Krissy had been carefree and mysterious, until Thursday after school. Then she had been busy as a hive full of bees until suppertime, even with Mom to help.

Now she carried the results of her work carefully packed in the cardboard box.

"But, Krissy," Sharon said again, "everybody gives Valentines."

"I didn't say I wasn't going to *give* any. I said I wasn't going to *send* any."

Sharon looked so puzzled that Krissy couldn't keep her secret any longer. "After all, it was you gave me the idea, Sharon," she said, untying the string on the box.

"Me?"

"Remember the poem in your magazine about the Valentreat? I told Mom. And she thought Valentarts would be a good idea, too . . . for the Queen of Hearts to give. So I made a Valentart for everyone in the room — a little heart-shaped cookie frosted in pink."

"Oh!" Sharon was impressed.

"I saved all the broken pieces for Skip," Krissy giggled. "A Valentart is the only kind of Valentine that means anything to a dog."

Krissy put her heart into the Valentine play that afternoon, and Mrs. Steele told her afterward that no one could have done better. And then, still dressed in her Queen costume, Krissy passed the Valentarts. Oh, it was a happy day leading up to Saturday. Leading up to taking Skip to the vet who would know what to do for his eyes.

But when Saturday actually came, Krissy felt trembly, the way she always felt when she faced something new and strange.

She held Skip next to her on the seat of the truck, held him close so Dad would have plenty of room for driving. Her head was dizzy with questions: Would the vet hurt Skip? Would it take long? Would Skip be scared? Would the vet be nice to him? Would Skip have to get medicine dropped in his eyes? Aloud she said, "Which vet is best for dogs, Dad?"

"We'll take Skip right to the animal hospital," Dad answered. "They'll know what to do. They mostly handle dogs there."

It was the first time Krissy had ever gone to the animal hospital. She didn't like the medicine smell or the sound of dogs barking in the kennels. She felt so shivery inside that her hands were stiff with cold. But she kept telling Skip everything was all right and saying, "Good boy, Skip."

They had to sit a few minutes in the waiting room. Then a man came out with a black-and-white spotted dog on a leash. "Just do what I said and she'll be all right in a day or two," someone called after him. "Don't worry."

"Don't worry, don't worry," Krissy said to herself, as if the words had been meant for her.

The vet wore a white jacket and glasses. He told Dad

and Krissy to bring Skip into another room. He patted Skip's head said, "Good boy, good boy." Then, gently, he lifted Skip to a shiny metal table. Krissy could tell he liked dogs.

Dad told about Skip's eyes, how there seemed to be a blue film over them. "It's been a couple of weeks now."

"Longer, Dad. Since the day you and Eric went to the Stock Show." But Krissy didn't contradict him out loud. She just waited and watched and kept her hand on one of Skip's paws, so he'd know she was there.

The vet held Skip's head toward the light and looked into his eyes, this way and that. Then he took a magnifying glass and looked again. He didn't say anything.

"Can you fix them?" Krissy whispered.

Finally the vet looked up, first at Krissy, then at Dad. He kept patting Skip's head. "It's just one of those things," he said.

"Nothing you can do?" Dad asked.

The vet shook his head.

"What about operating?"

The vet seemed sorry. "Dogs' eyes are very hard to operate on. There's a place in Boston that has had some success with operations of this kind."

"Boston!" Dad gave a grunt. "That's about as handy to Colorado as the South Pole."

"Even so, there'd be less than a fifty-fifty chance the dog could see again," the vet said. "We can't fit a dog with glasses, you know."

"Then . . . then . . ." Krissy couldn't say any more. She could feel her eyes burning, could see the vet's face turn fuzzy. She clutched at the little purse in her coat pocket. The junk money! All that money from the junk . . . and what good was it now?

The vet spoke to her gently. "I know you don't like to see a dog go blind. But it's nothing to feel so terribly sorry about. Because, you see, dogs can usually get along fine without eyes. I mean, the dog family isn't specially noted for good eyesight. They depend more on their sense of smell and hearing than on their eyes."

"Say it again," Krissy prayed. "Please say more, so Dad will be sure to hear."

"Your dog may bump into things for a while, but he'll sort of develop a sixth sense. Why, I even heard of a blind collie who was a good cow dog. I don't know how he did it, but he did."

"He did?" Krissy stole a look at Dad. But Dad had his doubts. They were sticking out all over his face.

The vet kept patting Skip. "You've got a beautiful dog here. He'll still be a good watchdog. I'm just sorry I can't do anything to bring his sight back."

"Well, that's that, then," Dad said, and reached for his billfold.

"I'm going to pay," Krissy said quickly. "I told you I'd pay, Dad." "Because I love Skip most," she added to herself, blinking. She took out her purse and looked at the vet. "How much is it?"

"Well, considering I couldn't really do anything for him — didn't even put drops in his eyes — it will just be two dollars." He put his hand on Krissy's shoulder. "And don't feel too bad about your dog. He's still a good dog."

"I know," Krissy said.

"But the trouble is Dad doesn't know," she cried inside. "He doesn't think Skip can pay his way. He doesn't think it's enough for Skip to bark when someone comes. He doesn't think a blind dog can be much good. But if he'll only give Skip a chance . . ."

The vet lifted Skip down from the shiny table.

"Thank you," Krissy gulped, guiding Skip out of the door.

"Well, that's that," Dad said again. "We can keep him for a while and see what happens."

FEBRUARY BLEW ITSELF AWAY, and March came. And soon the first day of spring was on the calendar. And Skip was still there — on trial!

"Dad's not saying anything yet. He's just sort of keeping Skip's record in his head," Krissy thought.

"Keep him a while and see what happens . . . keep him a while and see what happens." Dad's words were always in Krissy's mind, hanging there like a danger sign. How long was Dad willing to keep him and see?

At school that day, Mrs. Steele said, "Now that spring has officially started, let's start a new project. Let's have a Nature Discovery Table, like a little museum of interesting things from around here." She saw Philip waving his hand. "Yes, Philip?"

"Do you mean we should each discover something in nature and bring it to school?"

"Yes, something unusual. We've studied the common flowers and trees and stones. Now what about . . . well,

94

Indian things, for instance. I understand Indians used to camp north of town."

"What about an old grasshopper skin hanging from a weed?" Linda asked.

"That would be fine."

"Or a butterfly cocoon?"

"Excellent. If you can find one at this time of year." Mrs. Steele glanced out the window. Krissy knew the view by heart. Now the tips of the maple trees out there were bright with varnished buds, reddish brown. Behind them the sky was bluer than blue, and humping into the sky were the foothills showing the first tinge of green.

"A Colorado Nature Discovery Table," Mrs. Steele said, turning back. "When we get together a good exhibit, we can invite the other grades to come to see it."

Krissy and Sharon talked about it on the way home in the bus. "We have a better chance to find something than most of the others have," Krissy said, "since we live in the country. Maybe I can borrow Eric's hummingbird net. Except that he thinks it's worth a million dollars!"

"My little brother found a snakeskin last summer, and I think he kept it," Sharon said. "Imagine, the snake came right up to the stoop and rubbed against it to loosen the skin, and left it lying right there where we could step on it."

"A snakeskin would be good, Sharon. Especially if you put a note on it about the stoop."

"A yellow-jacket nest would be good too, but I'd hate to carry it to school," Sharon mused. "For fear the insides would come alive."

"I'm going to take Skip walking as soon as I get home," Krissy decided. "We'll go up the big gulch and see what we can find."

"But you never find anything when you're looking for it, Krissy!"

And that is the way it turned out.

The next day was cold and gray, swishing and swirling with wind. "I'm not going to look for anything today," Sharon said. "It's even hard to *see* when the wind blows."

"I'm going to. Maybe the wind will blow up something I wouldn't see otherwise." When she started something, Krissy didn't like to give up. She was going to keep looking until she found something for the Nature Discovery Table. "Maybe it will just swish up in front of me on such a windy day."

"If you don't swish away first," Sharon replied.

Krissy got off the bus and hurried through the gate, her skirt flipping and flapping. Where was Skip? He always came part way up the lane to meet her. Perhaps with the wind blowing he couldn't hear the bus stop. The air was too full of other sounds.

But Skip wasn't in the yard, either. Or in his box in the barn. Or at the corral.

Krissy went around calling and searching. "Here, Skip.

Here, Skip." The wind caught her voice and tossed it about like a straw, a wispy little straw. "Where are you, Skip?"

How empty the ranch looked and felt without Skip. Krissy ran to the house, scared and out of breath. Mom wasn't in the kitchen or the living room.

"Where *is* everyone?" Krissy called.

"Here," Mom answered. "In the storeroom, candling eggs."

Krissy burst into the dark room off the kitchen. There was Mom bundled up in a sweater, surrounded by eggs. "Where's Skip, Mom? Has anything happened to him?"

"Isn't he around, Krissy?"

"I can't find him anywhere." Krissy looked at Mom in fright. "Dad didn't . . . do anything to him, did he?"

"Why, no. Not that I know of."

"But maybe he wouldn't tell you," Krissy thought. "Because he knows you're on my side, Mom. Maybe he'd do it first and tell afterward. Maybe he'd think that was the easiest way. Like taking the kittens away from Blackie."

"Where did you look, Krissy?" Mom was asking.

"Everywhere. And it's all empty." "And I'm empty too," Krissy thought.

"Oh, he must be somewhere," Mom said confidently. She called out to Annie who was thumping around the kitchen being a pony for Carly. "Did you see Skip this afternoon, Annie? Try to remember."

"I didn't look," Annie called back. "It was too windy. Hold on tight, Carlie, 'cause the pony's going to buck."

Annie didn't care, and Carl didn't pay any attention. Verna, bending over the pattern that had come in the mail, didn't even listen. But Krissy cared enough for all of them.

"Perhaps he wandered off," Mom said. "Perhaps the wind brought a scent of something from the distance and he went after it. Then he couldn't find his way home again. It would be easy enough to get confused on a windy day like this."

Krissy remembered how her voice had blown away like a straw. "Yes, it would, Mom. Just so Dad didn't . . ."

"Oh, I'm sure he didn't," Mom assured her. "Go look some more. Perhaps Skip went to the gulch where it's more protected. Or maybe he's behind one of the sheds, out of the wind."

Krissy got into her jeans and Eric's old leather jacket, and went out into the wind again. "Skip! Skip!" But there was no Skip to be found! She headed for the gulch where they often walked, along the cow path. Here the wind was not so strong and her voice carried farther. "Skip! Here, Skip!"

Where was he? Why did he go wandering off on a day when scents and sounds scattered in all directions? Or didn't he wander off? Maybe Mom just didn't know . . .

The more Krissy searched and called, the more frightened she was. The more hollow she felt. A rabbit, jumping suddenly from its form under a low-spreading cedar, gave her a start. The loud swishing branches of the pines made her nervous. She seemed so all alone in an angry world. She never felt alone when Skip was there, no matter what the weather.

What would Dad say if Skip got lost?

Climbing to an open slope, Krissy turned back to face the east pasture. She cupped her hands around her face to keep the wind away. From here she had a good broad view . . . of emptiness. Wait! Something was moving out there in the pasture. Something too small for a cow, too big for a dog like Skip.

It was a girl, bent over against the wind! Sharon! And she hadn't even changed from her school dress. What was Sharon doing out in the wind when she said she wasn't going to look for anything for the Nature Discovery Table?

Krissy started running. She saw a quick movement in front of Sharon like a rabbit jumping. That must be Trigger. And then she saw another movement behind . . . a color that blended with the tawny grass. Could it be? Yes! It was Skip. Skip!

Oh, what a fullness all of a sudden where Krissy had felt so empty.

She ran ahead, calling. Her voice carried along toward Sharon. Sharon stopped and waved, and then they hurried toward each other. The wind was a friend now — a teasing, noisy friend that made Krissy feel full of joy.

"Where did you *find* him?" Krissy called. She didn't mind that her words flew apart before they reached Sharon. She didn't mind anything now. There was Skip, and that was all that mattered.

Sharon, who never liked to do anything fast, came up panting. "I knew you'd be worrying about Skip, Krissy. He must have followed Trigger home."

"Oh, Sharon."

Sharon was still out of breath. "Everything's so different in a wind. Mixed up like. Even when you can see. I guess Skip didn't know which way to go."

"You didn't even wait to change your dress," Krissy said.

"I knew you'd be looking for him. Worrying."

Krissy knelt down and put her arms around Skip. He was whole and real and alive! He nudged her face in that quick way he had and kissed her with his wet nose. "You scared me out of a year's growth," she scolded gently. "Two years'. But you've learned now, haven't you, Skip? You've learned you have to stay home on windy days. You can't go chasing Trigger."

She stood up again and looked at Sharon fondly. "You don't have to go right back, do you? Come home with me."

"I have to help my mother."

"Just come for a minute, Sharon. I want to give you something." Krissy linked her arm in Sharon's and urged her along. "Oh Sharon, I was so scared. I was afraid . . . something had happened. I thought I'd lost Skip and wouldn't ever see him again. And I felt so alone out there looking."

"I knew you'd be worrying," Sharon said, like a record going around.

"I want to give you something." The way Krissy felt, she'd give Sharon the moon and stars if she could. "I want to give you something real favorite. The little tea-pot, Sharon! It pours as good as new, even if there is that chip on the end of the spout."

# 13                                    Rain Check

Eric's birthday was the first of April. Dad always said, teasing, "Eric's my April fool."

Krissy wanted to get Eric a specially good birthday present this year, because he was always standing up for Skip. She still had some of the junk money, even after paying the vet and buying a green and pink bath mat for Mom's birthday. But she hoped she could think of a present for Eric that was more special than something she could buy for money.

Verna was thinking, too. "If it hadn't been for Eric," Verna said, "none of us would have been in on the Crag-horn gold mine! I want to think of something extra nice for his birthday."

Eric's birthday was always fun for everyone. Half his presents were "birthday" and the other half were April Fool; and he never knew when he opened one, which it would be.

"The trouble with me," Verna told Krissy, "is that I

have too many ideas. I don't know which to pick."

Too many ideas! Krissy didn't even have one.

"What ideas, Verna?"

"Well, in the first place, I want his present to have something to do with 4-H. He's so head-over-heels keen about 4-H."

Krissy nodded.

"I thought of embroidering the pledge in green on a background of white satin. But it's too long."

"Is it?"

"Five lines. Long ones, too, for embroidering." Verna shoved a piece of paper at Krissy and Krissy read:

I pledge my Head to clearer thinking,
My Heart to greater loyalty,
My Hands to larger service, and
My Health to better living, for
My Club, my Community, and my Country.

"Yes, it is long, isn't it?" Krissy agreed. "You couldn't get it all embroidered by the first of April. Why don't you do the motto instead, Verna? It's short."

"*To Make the Best Better*." Verna nodded, pursing her lips. "Maybe I will."

"Only Eric says it doesn't really apply to Lucky," Krissy remembered. "Because Lucky wasn't best to start with."

Verna hadn't thought of that angle, and she always got sort of huffy when she hadn't thought of something.

She tossed her head. "I think I'll go back to my original idea. The 4-H Club emblem. I'll sew a big, green satin four-leaf clover on a white background, and applique a white H on each leaf."

"He'll like that," Krissy said, "to hang in his room." She sighed. "I don't know what I'm going to give him. I haven't even *one* idea."

In the end she gave him a rain check, even though it wasn't raining on the first of April. She gave him a cardboard coupon with printing in black:

THIS IS GOOD FOR ONE VERY SPECIAL BIRTHDAY PRESENT WHEN I CAN THINK OF IT. I PROMISE TO THINK OF IT PRETTY SOON. LOVE FROM KRISSY.

But before Krissy thought of it, something happened at the Petersons' that gave everyone plenty to think about.

It happened the very day that Krissy and Eric told each other how well Skip was getting along. "He doesn't bump into things nearly as much as he used to," Krissy said.

"That's because he's got his radar set working," Eric explained. "He's getting to be like a bat."

"Like a *bat?*"

"Sure. Bats can race through a pitch-black night without bumping into anything. They make a high-pitched squeak when they fly, see? The sound bounces back if there's something in the way, and that warns them to turn aside."

"I never heard Skip make a high-pitched squeak, Eric."

"No, but when he get close to a tree or a boulder, air waves bounce back and warn him. It's the same idea."

"Good old Skip," Krissy thought. Even though he didn't carry his tail as high as he used to, sometimes he didn't act blind at all. Sometimes even Dad must see that Skip was practically as good as new.

That very night Dad came home with distressing news about the Petersons. "What we need around here is a dog with all his senses," he said. "Not one that can't see."

Krissy listened nervously. What did Dad mean?

"What's the matter, Dad?" Eric asked.

"Peterson lost two lambs this week. The first time he thought it was just an accident — a lamb straying off and getting caught in the rocks or something. But last night he lost the second. He thinks he saw bear tracks on the hill this morning."

"Bear tracks!" Mom exclaimed. "We haven't heard of a bear around here for years."

"Probably roamed down out of the hills when he woke up this spring, looking for something to eat. Though I think it's just as likely to be a mountain lion. It's tough on Peterson, losing those lambs," Dad said.

Krissy remembered the day she and Dad had gone for the aspen wood. "If I have good luck with the lambs,

I'll do all right," Mr. Peterson had said. But he wasn't having good luck with the lambs, was he? Losing two in one week.

"Gosh, Dad," Eric said, scared. "Do you think Lucky's safe? Could a bear or a mountain lion get Lucky, Dad?"

"Or Skip!" Krissy cried. "Could they get Skip?"

"I don't know what a bear or lion might do," Dad answered. "I just wish Peterson had a dog that could track the critter down. He's going to try a trap, but . . ." Dad shook his head, "I don't know."

"Oh, dear," Mom said. "There's always something, isn't there? Poor little lambs."

"Poor Peterson," Dad grunted.

The next week Eric got a job.

Dad found out there was going to be one down at the feed store, and he asked the manager to hold the place for Eric. It was only part-time work for two weeks — after school and on Saturdays — while one of the men took a vacation. But it paid well.

Eric was excited. "The way Lucky keeps eating and growing and eating some more, I can use a job. I can stand getting a little money ahead, now that there isn't any more junk to sell."

"Antiques!" Verna corrected.

"You'll have to stay in town, Eric," Mom said. "The Craghorns have an extra room, and I'm sure they'll be glad to have you. I'll call Grace . . ."

Eric hadn't thought that far ahead. "But if I have to stay in town, what about Lucky? Who's going to take care of Lucky? He has to be fed just so, and he has to be kept in training or he'll forget all he knows."

"The rain check!" Krissy exclaimed.

Eric looked blank. So did everyone else.

"Your rain-check birthday present," Krissy went on eagerly. "I wanted to think of something different and special. And this is it, Eric. I'll take care of Lucky for your birthday present, and keep the records, and brush him, and lead him around. I'll take real good care of him. It's a promise."

"Gosh, Kris," Eric said, taking the coupon from his pocket. "All that for one present? Gosh, I won't have to worry about Lucky at all!"

Krissy was eager to get started. It would be fun measuring out Lucky's food each day and seeing that there was water in the trough and salt in the box; six pounds of corn, five pounds of hay, three pounds of silage with molasses in it, two pounds of barley, one pound of cottonseed meal. It would be fun brushing Lucky till his burnished hair lay smooth and clean. And leading him around the corral, holding tight to the rope, the way Eric did.

Krissy smiled happily. Now both Skip and Lucky would depend on her!

# 14                    Krissy Takes Over

THE FIRST SATURDAY Eric was working at the feed store, someone unexpectedly came to see him. Krissy was helping Mom weed the flower beds.

It was the kind of morning that sang — so bright and calm, so blue and green. In the pines, robins were busy looking over building prospects. A pair of mountain bluebirds were back at the birdhouse, peeking in, flying away, and coming back to look again. Krissy wondered if they had nested there last year.

She was talking to Mom about the subject that weighed heaviest on her mind — Skip. "Has Dad said anything about Skip lately, Mom?" His silence was hard to bear because it was so uncertain.

Mom was separating a mass of iris roots, getting some ready to plant in another bed. The others were for Mrs. Moss, who had moved into the Craghorn house. "Well, not *very* lately."

"When?" Krissy wanted to know.

"A few weeks ago."

"What did he say, Mom?"

They were close together, the two of them, working in the warm earth in the spring sunshine. And *feeling* close together, too. Annie and Carl had piled some cardboard cartons behind the clump of lilac bushes and were playing house. Verna was sewing, and the old sewing machine behind the window sounded like a swarm of insects. Dad was off somewhere. It was his busiest time — the time for looking after the new calves, and getting the fields ready for planting. Eric was down at the feed store, earning grain and molasses for his catch-it calf. It was as if Krissy and Mom inhabited a little island all their own.

"What did Dad say, Mom?" Krissy asked again when Mom hesitated.

"Well . . . one day he took a load of hay to the Maxwells'. There was a litter of pups there — shepherds — four or five weeks old. Mr. Maxwell said the mother was a good cow dog, and he offered Dad one of the pups."

Krissy gasped. She stopped digging and stared at Mom.

"Dad was tempted," Mom went on. "He told me he thought he might make something out of one of the pups."

"And keep Skip, too?" Krissy breathed.

"I'm afraid not, Krissy. Dad can't see much sense in having two dogs."

"Oh, Mom! There can't be a better dog than Skip!"

"I know, Krissy. And I feel sorry for him, too. But Dad's afraid he isn't much good any more, except to bark when someone comes. How can Skip keep the cows away from the trees and shrubbery when they're in this pasture? That's what Dad wants to know. It's out of the question to put up another fence, with posts costing more than a dollar apiece, to say nothing of the wire and Dad's time."

"Can't Dad keep this pasture for summer, Mom? When I'm here to help Skip? Can't he, Mom?"

"That's just what I suggested, Krissy."

Krissy's heart beat a few extra strokes . . . for Mom. "What did he say?" Krissy asked, trembling. She put out her hand to pat Skip lying nearby, dozing in the sunlight.

"He said there wasn't any hurry. Said the puppies were too small anyway to do much with now. So there's no use worrying about it *yet*, Krissy."

"But the *yet* never lasts," Krissy cried inside herself. "Next month it is gone and *now* is in its place. And what will Dad think when *now* arrives? Will he still think he can make a cow dog out of one of Mr. Maxwell's pups?"

Skip suddenly raised his head and cocked his ears. Then he jumped up, alert in every muscle, his nose pointed toward the road, his tail waving nervously. He began to bark his watchdog bark.

Both Krissy and Mom looked toward the road. A clump of pines kept them from seeing the gate, but they heard a car start and stop, heard a door bang. Someone was getting out to close the gate. Skip kept barking.

"Someone's coming," Mom said, "Skip always knows. How's my hair, Krissy?"

A blue and gray car, with the sun sparkling on the chromium, came swinging down the lane. Krissy didn't recognize it. Skip ran ahead, barking.

"Come back, Skip. Come back!" Krissy called.

"See who it is," Mom said. "If it's that spice-and-extract man, tell him I don't need a thing today. If it's someone for Dad, he won't be home till noon."

Krissy hurried toward the shiny car. A man was getting out — a youngish man in a tweed jacket and without a hat. She had never see him before.

"I'm looking for a boy named Eric Ohling," the man said. "Is this the place? Looks like Ohling on the mailbox, but the letters aren't clear."

The letters were faded, Krissy knew. Mom always said they should be painted on again, big and black. But nobody ever seemed to get around to it. "Eric isn't here," Krissy said. "He's got a job down at the feed store. Just for two weeks though."

The young man was looking around, at the barn, at the corral. "That's too bad. I hoped Eric would show me his calf. I understand he's one of the 4-H boys who got a catch-it calf at the Stock Show this year."

"Oh yes," Krissy said proudly. "He was the youngest boy to catch one. He was only thirteen then."

"So I hear. You're his sister?"

Krissy nodded. "I'm Krissy. I know all about the calf. I'm taking care of it for Eric while he's working." She patted Skip's head as she talked. Whenever she stopped, he nudged her, wanting more.

"That's a nice dog. Is he yours?"

"Mostly."

"You're a busy girl, aren't you?" the man said with a smile. "Which do you like best, dogs or calves?"

"Oh, they're so different," Krissy answered quickly. "A dog is . . . well, he's a person. And a calf isn't. I mean, you can like a calf, but he doesn't have feelings about you, the way a dog does." Krissy didn't quite know how to say it. She tried again. "I like the catch-it calf, but I love Skip."

"I see what you mean," the man said. "Well, if you know all about Eric's calf, perhaps you can give me some of the facts I need for my story. Then I can check with Eric when I get back to town."

"Are you writing a *story?*"

"An article. A little human-interest article for the newspaper. I'm a reporter, you see. I meant to run up here before, but I never had time. But better late than never!"

Krissy was excited — an article about Eric and Lucky in the newspaper! "I'll show you the calf," she offered eagerly. Then she called out to Mom. "The man wants to see Lucky," and they headed for the corral.

Krissy put Lucky through his paces. "You sit on the top rail," she told the man, "and be the judge — like at

the Stock Show. This is the arena." She put a halter on
Lucky and led him around by the rope. He was quite
tame by now and didn't pull back once. Then she made
Lucky stand, the way Eric had taught him to. She tapped
his feet with Eric's long stick until they were just right,
squarely under him.

"If I'd known you were coming," she said, "I would
have had him all spruced up. Washed and curled. And
his hoofs polished."

The reporter laughed. "He still looks pretty good."

"He was only C grade when Eric caught him," Krissy
explained. "But he'll be C plus . . . or maybe even B
by next January."

"I'm sure he will. How much does he weigh?"

Krissy didn't have to look at the record sheets. She
knew it all by heart. "He weighed 415 pounds when
Eric brought him home from the National Western, and
he weighed 565 pounds last week when Eric took him
to the feed store to be weighed. That's a gain of 150
pounds in two and a half months."

"So it is," said the reporter, noting down the figures.

"Eric wants him to gain two pounds a day, and that's
just about what he's doing. Eric knows all about fatten-
ing a calf. He learned it in 4-H."

"You just feed him a lot, isn't that the idea?"

"A lot of the *right things*," Krissy corrected. "You can't
just stuff him with hay. You have to give him grain and
silage, and if you put molasses on, he likes it even better."

"Smart calf," the young man said. He wanted to see everything. Krissy showed him the records: how much Lucky ate, how much the food cost, how much he weighed every month.

"One of the farm magazines in Denver sponsored Lucky," she explained. "Eric has to send them a report once a month. He says that's the hardest part of catching a calf, writing the report." She looked up and smiled. "I guess he'd never do for a reporter!"

"Not any more than I'd want to tussle with 415 pounds of calf at a stock show." The young man made a few more notes. "Well, thanks, Krissy. I can see the catch-it calf is in good hands."

"I'd catch it if anything happened to Lucky," Krissy said, her eyes twinkling.

"And I'll catch it if I don't get back to the office," came the quick reply.

Krissy told the reporter where to find Eric, as they walked to the car. "Thanks again," the nice young man said as he got in. "And take good care of that calf."

"Oh, I will," Krissy said. She watched the shiny car go up the lane, heard the reporter toot another good-bye. Then she turned back to Mom and the iris bed. "Won't Eric be pleased," she thought, "to be written up in the paper? Won't Dad be surprised?" She walked along thoughtfully. "I wonder . . . I wonder if *I'll* ever be important enough to get my name in the paper."

# 15                                    Black Friday

KRISSY FOLLOWED VERNA down the lane from the school bus after Verna stopped at the mailbox. Krissy never wrote letters, except thank-you notes for Christmas or birthday presents. She never expected to get any mail. But this Thursday she was surprised!

Verna couldn't believe her eyes. "There's nothing for anyone but you, Krissy."

"For me?" Krissy couldn't believe it either.

Verna handed her a letter and a newspaper with a slip of brown wrapper around it.

"Two things for *me?*"

"Open the letter," Verna urged. "I can't imagine why anyone would be writing to you. Read what it says."

Krissy fondled the envelope. Her name and address were typed on the front. Maybe it was just an ad. Maybe Sharon had sent in her name for something. Maybe it wasn't important at all. "I'm not going to open it just yet," she told Verna.

Krissy took Skip out to the corral and there, leaning

against the rails, she tore open one end of the envelope. There was a little typewritten slip inside:

> Dear Krissy: Just a note to thank you again. I wrote up the article and I'm sending you a copy under separate cover. I hope you won't mind that I quoted you on a few things. Take good care of Lucky!

The reporter had signed his name in such a scrawl that Krissy couldn't even read it.

Eagerly she opened the paper, looking for ERIC and CATCH-IT CALF in the headlines. There was nothing on the first page, or the second, or the third. The fourth page was all society news, so it wouldn't be there. Then came two pages of sports. Well, they might count it a sport to catch a wild little calf. But no, it wasn't there.

On page seven there was a broad headline over two columns with the word KRISSY in it. She read eagerly:

KRISSY DIDN'T CATCH THE CATCH-IT BUT SHE'LL
CATCH IT IF ANYTHING HAPPENS TO THE CATCH-IT.

Eric was mentioned in the first paragraph and at the end, and 4-H Club and National Western Stock Show were scattered here and there, but the article was mostly about Krissy. Krissy taking over for her brother while he earned money for feed. Krissy showing off the catch-it calf to the "judge" on the corral fence. Krissy explaining how to feed a calf to make it fat. Krissy rattling off the figures . . .

"Oh, Skip," Krissy cried. "I'm in the paper! Look, I'm

right here in the paper." She caught herself. Skip couldn't see, and he wouldn't know what it was all about if he could. But he could hear. He could hear that something exciting had happened.

"I never thought I'd do anything worth putting in the paper," she went on happily. "And there I am. Now I've got to take better care of Lucky than ever. I've got to make him *shine* for Eric when he comes home Saturday night. Oh, Skip, let's go show Mom and Verna."

Some days are made of gold, Krissy thought as she ran toward the house. Like today!

Dad came home at suppertime with the news that Mr. Peterson had lost another lamb. But no one had time to talk about their neighbor's hard luck. Dad must see the paper. Dad must read the article aloud. Dad must be surprised — and he was!

Next morning at school was made of gold, too. Philip brought a copy of the paper, and Mrs. Steele read the article to the class. Krissy kept looking down at the book on her desk, but inside she had a nice, excited feeling.

And coming home from school was gold-plated too, with Sharon sitting next to Krissy and looking so proud.

"I'll get Skip and walk over to see the colt," Krissy said. "I haven't seen him for a long time. And it's such a lovely day, isn't it, Sharon? Look at the green beginning to come into the hills. And look at the tops of those willows along the gulch. Yellow as fire." Not that fire is yellow, Krissy told herself. But it's living. And that's the way with the willow tops.

Krissy was surprised on the way down the lane from the gate when Verna said that she was going for a walk, too. Verna hardly ever went for walks.

"I want to find some feathers," she explained. "I want to try to make a feather belt."

"What kind of feathers?" asked Krissy.

"Colored ones. Not just white like Mom's chickens. I want some feathers with character."

"Do magpie feathers have character, Verna?"

"Oh, I should say. Black and white? Definitely."

"I saw some in the corral," Krissy said. "I even saw a magpie riding around on Lucky's back the other day. They like to come to the corral to peck around. And what about blue jays' feathers? Do they have character?"

"Of course, Krissy." Verna was already designing the feather belt. "Black and white and blue-jay blue! Nobody will have a belt like that. If I can only work it out."

"I saw some blue-jay feathers over by the first gulch in the west pasture. The jays must have had a fight. They're near some rocks under a pine tree, where the cow path crosses the gulch."

"Good," said Verna. "I'll pick up the magpie feathers in the corral, then go for the blue ones. The first gulch?"

Krissy nodded. "In the west pasture, toward the big hill."

So Verna went to the corral for the magpie feathers, and Krissy and Skip hurried off to the Petersons' ranch.

Krissy got home later than she expected. She hurried right to the corral to give Lucky his brushing before leading him around. He liked to be brushed. And he was very good these days about the halter and the rope.

Funny, Lucky was usually up near the bars, waiting for her. But this Friday afternoon he was nowhere to be seen. Krissy called eagerly, "Where are you, Lucky? Don't you want a brushing? Come on, Lucky."

He didn't come out from the little shed that opened into the corral. He couldn't have wandered into the big west pasture because that gate was always kept closed.

Krissy had an awful thought. Was Lucky sick? Had he eaten something that didn't agree with him? Was he lying in the shed unable to move?

She slipped through the corral poles and ran to the shed. There was the rope and halter hanging from a peg. There was the straw for Lucky's bed, and the training stick. But no calf. Not a sign of him anywhere.

Suddenly Krissy remembered what Dad had said the night before, when they were all so excited over the article. "Peterson's lost another lamb," Dad had said.

Could a black bear or a mountain lion kill a calf as big as Lucky? Drag him through the poles of the corral? Or over the top? "Oh!" Krissy gasped just to think of it. All the shine was gone from the day. Now fear made everything look as black as midnight.

Where was Dad? What could they do? What would Eric say? *What* had happened to Lucky? "Dad! Dad!" Krissy cried, as she slipped out of the corral and ran toward the barn. "DAD!"

# 16                                      The Search

D AD WASN'T IN THE BARN and the truck was gone.
Krissy didn't know what to do. To think that something like this should happen when she was giving Eric
his special birthday present! "I'll take real good care of
Lucky," she had said. "It's a promise."

Real good care of Lucky! And where was he now?
Where was he?

She thought of the article in the paper. The headline: KRISSY DIDN'T CATCH THE CATCH-IT BUT
SHE'LL CATCH IT . . .

"Dad!" Krissy called again at the top of her voice.
"Dad!"

Skip was staring toward the road with his sightless
eyes, waving his tail. Krissy heard a car stop, but Skip
didn't bark. That must mean it was Dad coming home.
Skip knew the sound of the truck and never barked at it.

Yes, there was Dad driving in with a load of silage.
Krissy ran to meet him, signaling him to stop. "Dad,"
she gasped, "Lucky's gone! Eric's calf is gone!"

Dad couldn't believe it. He had to hop out to see for himself. "How can he be gone, Krissy?" he asked, hurrying to the corral. There wasn't a sign of Lucky. Dad looked at Krissy, baffled.

"Nobody was home for almost two hours, Dad. I went over to Sharon's with Skip as soon as I got home from school. And Verna went hunting feathers. And Mom left a note that Mrs. Moss had taken her and the kids to a tea party. Do you think . . . a bear or a mountain lion could have got him when nobody was here, Dad?"

"I can't believe it. Not in broad daylight. Not so close to the house."

"Where *is* he then?" Krissy was afraid she was going to cry. What would Eric say?

"You sure the gate was closed, Krissy?" Dad asked. "If Lucky got in to the west pasture, heaven only knows where he might wander. There's two hundred and forty acres in that pasture, running up and down the hills. It's two and a half miles around the fence."

Krissy shaded her eyes against the sun and looked toward the hills. If Lucky got into the west pasture, he'd be as hard to find as a tadpole in a mud puddle. He might fall into an old mine hole and break his neck, or a leg. He might slip on the rocks. Lucky was a feed-lot calf; he didn't know anything about pastures or mine holes.

"But, Dad," Krissy pointed out, "the gate's closed. Look, it's closed. How could Lucky get out of the corral?"

"That's what we have to find out. I'll check the poles.

You walk around and see if you see any strange tracks."
Dad started to go, and almost tripped over Skip. Krissy
saw him frown. She knew what Dad was thinking: Now
if we only had a good cow dog instead of one that can't
even see.

Krissy couldn't see any strange tracks, and Dad
couldn't find anything wrong with the poles. There wasn't
a single place where Lucky could squeeze through.

"When was the last time you saw him, Krissy?"

"Before I went to Sharon's. I rubbed his nose. He was
standing in the shed in the shade. Verna probably didn't
even notice him when she was looking for the feathers."

"Verna? Feathers? What feathers?"

Krissy told Dad about the feather belt.

"Look here," Dad said. "If Verna had a feather belt on
her mind . . . Where is she? Go get her, Krissy. Bring her
here."

Krissy went on the run.

Yes, Verna had been in the corral and had picked up a
few magpie feathers. Yes, she had gone straight from
the corral to the west pasture, along the gulch, to find
the jay feathers. It had taken her quite a while. She
didn't remember about the gate. Yes, she did, too. She remembered closing it when she came back, because she
thought it strange that it was open.

"It was open because you left it open, Verna," Dad
scolded. "A girl with feather belts on her mind shouldn't
be fooling around with gates."

"Needles and thread, patterns and belts," Krissy thought. *Now* what were they going to do? Verna had left the gate open, and Lucky had wandered out into the west pasture, and it would soon be dark!

"I'm sorry," Verna said. "But I didn't even see Lucky when I went through the corral. I was looking for feathers . . ."

Dad tried to console Krissy. "Don't worry, Krissy. Lucky knows where the feed box is. He'll come home when he's hungry."

But Lucky didn't come home! After gulping down her supper, Krissy sat on the top rail of the corral and waited and waited. Lucky didn't come. It was long past feeding time, but still he didn't come. "He'll lose weight," She kept telling Skip. "He has to gain two pounds a day, and he hasn't even had any supper."

After a while Verna came, and tried to be cheerful. "Of course, he'll find his way back when he gets hungry enough, Krissy. He's not dumb."

"But oh, Verna . . ." Krissy couldn't help spilling out the fears that tormented her. "All alone there in the pasture, Lucky wouldn't have a chance if a bear or a mountain lion came. Dad says they wouldn't dare come so close to the house in broad daylight. But out there! And I told Eric I'd take good care of his calf."

"Oh, bother. Bother catch-it calves, anyway. You shouldn't have told me about those feathers in the corral, Krissy." Verna stalked off into the night.

Krissy trembled. Was Verna putting the blame on her, then?

In a moment Verna's voice floated back dramatically. "Don't worry. *I'll* take the blame."

Finally Dad came out and made Krissy go to bed. "We can't do anything about it in the dark," he said persuasively. "Tomorrow's Saturday. We'll get up early and hunt till we find him. We've got to find him before Eric comes home to spend Sunday."

All night long the old wheel clicked around in Krissy's head. But this time the name on the spokes wasn't *Skip*. It was *Lucky*. Lucky . . . Lucky . . . Lucky . . . clicking round and round.

They started hunting right after an early breakfast, all except Annie and Carl. Dad and Mom went on horseback. Verna was to follow the gulch on the right, Krissy and Skip the gulch on the left.

"He might have found the other cows and joined the herd," Dad said. "Maybe he was lonesome. I'll check on that first thing."

"I'll cover the mine holes,'" Mom said.

For hours they searched the west pasture. Lucky wasn't with the other cows. He hadn't fallen into a hole. He wasn't in the gulches. He wasn't anywhere!

Krissy got more and more nervous as the morning passed. Three times she hurried back to the corral to see if Lucky had come. Three times she was disappointed.

"I can't understand it," Dad said when she met him

near the gulch. "I was sure he'd find his way back when he got hungry enough. He's used to something much better than last year's grass and a few sprigs of green. Fortunately there's water in the gulches at this time of year."

"He didn't have any supper or any breakfast." Krissy hesitated, full of fear. "Dad, do you think the bear got him?"

"I'll think that only as a last resort. Let's do some more looking."

In the middle of the morning Krissy traded gulches with Verna so they could check on each other. Verna was tired to death, but persistent. "Poor Eric," she kept saying. "What's he going to say when he comes home tonight? Poor *me*, for leaving that gate open."

Krissy and Skip trudged up the gulch. A little stream of water ran through the rocks, sparkling with sunlight. Skip could drink it, but Krissy knew it wasn't safe for her . . . and she was so thirsty her mouth seemed full of cotton.

The day was hot for April, and she was tired. The brambles scratched. Skip stepped on a cactus plant, and Krissy tried to get the stickers out from between his toes. She found it hard to keep from crying. Everything was going wrong.

Then suddenly she heard Dad shouting and her heart leapt with relief. Dad must have found Lucky! His voice seemed to come from near the fence between their ranch and the Petersons'. Maybe Lucky had just been curious, like most animals, and strayed over there to look at the karakul sheep. He'd probably never seen any before.

"Come on, Skip," Krissy urged, hurrying toward Dad's voice beyond a rise of ground. Her legs were no longer heavy, her face no longer hot. She was full of eager energy again, and hope. Good for Dad to find Lucky!

But Dad had not found Lucky. When Krissy reached him, he had already turned away from the fence and was continuing the search. "Didn't you *find* him?" Krissy called.

Dad rode toward Krissy and stopped the horse. "Haven't seen hide or hair of Lucky."

She slumped against a tree. "I heard you shouting, and I thought you'd found him," she sighed.

Dad shook his head. "Just shouting to Peterson. I saw him on the hill. He's rushing back to get John Maxwell to help him trail the bear."

So the bear was still around! Had he found Lucky? Krissy's voice trembled. "Oh, Dad . . ."

"I don't think they'll have too much trouble finding the bear," Dad went on confidently. "Know what that bear did, Krissy? Walked off with Peterson's trap! The critter can't make very good time that way. Well, we'd better get going. Try Verna's gulch again. Her head was probably full of feathers."

# 17 A Real Good Dog

Krissy trudged back up the scraggly gulch. She couldn't believe that the world had looked so bright just a few minutes ago, when she heard Dad's shout. Now everything was heavy and hot again.

What if the reporter found out about this? she thought with horror. She could just see the headline: KRISSY FINDS A CATCH-IT EASIER TO CATCH THAN TO KEEP. Something like that. Something that tried to be funny. Oh, she didn't like reporters, she decided.

She felt hot and itchy all over. Nothing was right. Even the pasqueflowers looked dowdy, faded, past their prime. Little clumps of Easter daisies, buttoned close to the gravelly ground, were still fresh and bright, but they failed to kindle the usual spark of joy.

"Oh, Skip," she sighed for the hundredth time, "where's Lucky? Where's Lucky, Skip?"

She looked around. She had been talking to the empty air. Skip wasn't there! He wasn't following her, though she remembered seeing him just a few minutes before when they had scrambled over a rough place. "Skip!"

she called desperately. "Here, Skip!" Now what if Skip
got lost, too? Dad had told her she was foolish to take
him. "It's hard enough walking in a gulch when you can
see," Dad said. "It's a lot worse when you can't."

"Here, Skip! Here, Skip!" Krissy was more frightened
now than ever.

She looked up at the tangle of wild plum trees and
wild cherries on the bank, behind a fringe of brambly
gooseberries and wild currant bushes. The thorny
plum branches were full of buds on the verge of breaking
into fragrant bloom. Here and there buds were actually
open, shaking themselves out after being packed in so
tight. The cherries were just coming into leaf.

"I can't get up on the bank there," Krissy thought.
"Not in all that tangle." She turned back. She had to find
Skip somehow. She called again. And again.

Now an answering yip came from the brambles farther
down the gulch. It wasn't Skip's rabbit bark.

She hurried along, climbing to the bank through
scratchy gooseberry bushes and gnarled roots. "Skip!"
She ducked her head and pushed through the tangle of
plum trees. "Skip, where are you?" Ahead she could see
the white of his tail waving back and forth. "Oh, Skip,
how did you get in there? Can't you find your way out?"

And then . . . could she believe it? She saw something
else move. Something red and white, just beyond Skip.
Could it be? Could it possibly be? Yes, it was Lucky!

"Skip found him!" Krissy cried to her pounding heart.
"Skip can't *see*, but he found Lucky!"

Making her way through the thorny branches, Krissy saw why Lucky hadn't come home for supper, why he hadn't come home for breakfast, why he looked so forlorn. He was caught. The brush of his tail was caught on the plum thorns. He must have flipped his tail and got it snagged on a brambly branch, and then the more he pulled to free himself, the worse the snarl became.

"Oh, Lucky, Lucky!" Krissy gave Skip a pat as she passed, and rubbed Lucky's poor hot face. Carefully, gently, she worked the brush of his tail off the thorns. Then she rubbed his tail to get some life back into it.

Poor Lucky. He must have ventured into the tangle yesterday afternoon to find some shade. How would a corral calf know that wild plums had thorns? How could he know that he might get caught?

Krissy had brought a rope, looped around her waist. Now she put it around Lucky's neck, and slowly led him from the thicket to the cow path on the side of the slope.

"Poor thing," she said. "I bet you've never been so hungry or thirsty in your life. Wait till we get to the corral."

She saw Skip following along happily, carrying his tail high. Good old Skip. Now they were out in the open. Krissy could see Dad on horseback, down below, near the end of the gulch. She yelled and yelled, and waved her free hand. Skip barked.

Dad turned and waved, and came riding up the slope.

"Oh Dad, Dad," Krissy called, "Skip found him. Can you hear? Skip found Lucky in the thicket!"

"Where?" Dad yelled, cupping his ear to listen.

"In the plum thicket, Dad. Up on the bank. He was caught — his tail was caught. Skip found him!"

Dad jumped off his horse to take a look at Lucky's tail. "I've heard of cows losing their tails, getting hung up by them. Lucky wouldn't make much of a show at the National Western next winter without a tail. But he seems to be all right, Krissy. It's lucky you found him in time."

"*Skip* found him, Dad. I passed by there a couple of times. So did Verna. Skip must have got his scent."

Dad reached down and patted Skip on the head. Krissy watched, blinking the mist from her eyes.

"You're a good dog, Skip," Dad said. "You're a real good dog." Then he looked at Krissy with a sort of smile. "You win, Krissy."

That was all he said. But it was enough. Krissy trembled with joy now, not fear. Dad had called Skip a good dog. A real good dog. And Dad had said, "You win, Krissy." She ventured a look at his face. There weren't any doubts sticking out on it now, the way there had been all along.

"I'll go tell the others," Dad said quickly, swinging himself up into the saddle. "They'll want to know."

Krissy ran ahead on the path, leading Lucky by the rope. Skip ran beside her. His tail was curving high over his back, like a showery waterfall. The way it used to!

"Oh, Skip," Krissy cried, feeling light as a butterfly. "Did you hear what Dad said? Do you know what it means? Lucky isn't the only lucky one! We're lucky too. Everything's going to be all right now for you and me."